"In *Somewhere Fast*, Bob does a great job showing us the discovery of a moral compass. This is a worthwhile read!"

— PHILIP ANSCHUTZ
chairman and CEO, Anschutz Corporation

"A fugitive from his broken past and his God, a man rides his Harley on a journey that proves to be a pursuit by the Hound of Heaven. A universal plot is retold in a contemporary idiom that makes this odyssey grippingly relevant."

— DR. VERNON C. GROUNDS
chancellor, Denver Seminary

"*Somewhere Fast* completely captured me from beginning to end. Bob Beltz wrote a sure best seller. I enthusiastically recommend this wild, winding, winsome read to you!"

— WALT KALLESTAD
minister, Community Church of Joy; author; biker

"Bob Beltz beautifully synchronizes spirituality with nature, Americana, and the desire to find peace through travel, expertly capturing a possible road map to salvation. Through stunning descriptions and enlightening insights, *Somewhere Fast* is a truly inspiring tale that will aid many wayward souls in finding their personal grace."

— COLLEEN CAMP
actress; producer

"Packed with meaning and told as a parable, this fictional encounter is filled with questions posed and wisdom gained in the Halftime/Second Half season of a man's life. It is a remarkable journey, a tale well told."

— BOB BUFORD
author, *Halftime and Finishing Well*; founder, Leadership Network

D0048162

"The crucial journey toward personal and spiritual genuineness is the worthy road trip of *Somewhere Fast*. Bob Beltz has captured the reality and the revelation of making the second-half turn after first-half failures. He leads us on the back of John Calvin's Harley Davidson road king on a ride of self-discovery and profound spiritual insight. Every man navigating his own life-crisis moments would do well to read and learn from the route *Somewhere Fast* follows."

— DAVID PARKER
senior pastor, Desert Vineyard Church

"I found this story of one man's crisis of faith very entertaining and a great read."

— MR. TALL JOHN ROELFSEMA
manager, Rocky Mountain Harley-Davidson Motor Company

"In addition to developing a desire to cruise Route 66, I had many of my own life questions answered in this capturing, must-read novel of prophetic proportion."

— DR. WAYNE CORDEIRO
senior pastor, New Hope Church

"Bob Beltz has brought great humor and true insight into the "journey" of self-realization that all American men must embark on. His protagonist's discoveries are those of all of us; however, Beltz reveals them with the true talent of a gifted writer."

— MARK JOHNSON
producer, *The Lion, the Witch and the Wardrobe*;
Academy Award-winning producer of *Rain Man*, *The Natural*,
The Rookie, *The Alamo*, and *The Notebook*

BOB BELTZ

Somewhere Fast

a novel

NAVPRESS®

BRINGING TRUTH TO LIFE

OUR GUARANTEE TO YOU

We believe so strongly in the message of our books that we are making this quality guarantee to you. If for any reason you are disappointed with the content of this book, return the title page to us with your name and address and we will refund to you the list price of the book. To help us serve you better, please briefly describe why you were disappointed. Mail your refund request to: NavPress, P.O. Box 35002, Colorado Springs, CO 80935.

NavPress
P.O. Box 35001
Colorado Sprinigs, CO 80935

© 2005 by Robert L. Beltz

ISBN 1-57683-625-8

Cover design by Charles Brock, The DesignWorks Group, Inc., www.thedesignworksgroup.com
Cover image by Photonica
Creative team: Terry Behimer, Dave Lambert, Arvid Wallen, Darla Hightower, Glynese Northam
Author photo by Mary Robinson

This novel is a work of fiction. Names, characters, places, and incidents are either the product of the author's imagination or are used fictitiously.

Any resemblance to actual events, locales, organizations, or persons, living or dead, is entirely coincidental and beyond the intent of either the author or publisher.

Beltz, Bob.
  Somewhere fast / Bob Beltz.
    p. cm.
  ISBN 1-57683-625-8
  1. Middle aged men--Fiction. 2. Harley-Davidson motorcycle--Fiction. 3. United States
Highway 66--Fiction. 4. Quests (Expeditions)--Fiction. 5. Spiritual life--Fiction. 6.
Motorcyclists--Fiction. 7. Motorcycling--Fiction. 8. Travelers--Fiction. I. Title.
  PS3602.E653E55 2005
  813'.6--dc22
                          2004025050

Published in association with Eames Literary Services, Nashville, Tennessee.

Printed in Canada

1 2 3 4 5 6 7 8 9 10 / 09 08 07 06 05

FOR A FREE CATALOG OF
NAVPRESS BOOKS & BIBLE STUDIES,
CALL 1-800-366-7788 (USA)
OR 1-800-839-4769 (CANADA)

for

Ali

Acknowledgments

Somewhere Fast could not have been written without the help of a small army of people who have influenced my life through the years and taught me things that are so intertwined with the story that it is nearly impossible to give credit where credit is due.

I first encountered Richard Rohr many years ago. I had read his books, listened to his tapes, and benefited from his work for almost ten years before I finally had the chance to spend a week with him at Ghost Ranch in northern New Mexico. His way of taking the great spiritual teachers of the past and putting their ideas in a contemporary context provided much of the spiritual journey material contained in the book. His encouragement to share what we learned — however we could — inspired me to set the journey within the context of a novel. I would be remiss if I acknowledged Richard without thanking St. John of the Cross and Teresa of Avila, among others, for providing "shoulders to stand on."

Frank Timmons, David Becker, Doug Fiel, Vernon Grounds, and most of all Bryan Van Draught contributed to helping me grasp the psychological dimensions that permeate the book. My twenty-one days of solitude on Fox Island, directed by Bryan, were life-changing days, without which this book never could have been written.

I'm grateful to Dick Savidge for getting me back on a motorcycle after nearly twenty years of not touching one. The guys at Rocky Mountain Harley Davidson—Tall John, Vinny, Ron, Marc, Tom, Troy, and Kathy (not really one of the guys)—have not only helped me keep the rubber side down, but have also been great friends.

Thank you, Phil, for giving me a "day job." It's been a fun ride.

Without the love, support, encouragement, and commitment of my wife, Allison, it is entirely possible that this book could have been autobiographical instead of fictional. Along with my son, Baker, and my daughter, Stephanie, she has been my refuge from the storm.

Finally, without God being God, I'm quite sure I couldn't get out of bed in the morning, much less string together any words that make sense. Thank you, Father.

P.S. Thanks to Dave Lambert, Terry Behimer, Kent Wilson, and all the crew at NavPress for all their help.

Illinois

Journal — September 11: I once heard someone say that a man spends the first forty-five years of his life building a tower — only to discover that he has built it against the wrong wall. It somehow seems fitting that I'm starting this journey on 9/11, the anniversary of the day the towers came down. It's been years since that day, and yet the sight of those towers crumbling to the ground is an image as vivid in my mind today as it was then. It is an image that provides the perfect metaphor for the last five years of my life.

I find that the hardest part of telling a story like this is to figure out where and how to start. The Chinese philosopher Lao Tzu is credited with coining the expression that a journey of a thousand miles begins with a single step. Sound wisdom, unless you happen to be standing on the edge of a precipice when you take it. I was.

Maybe the best place to start is with the dream. It is a recurring one.

DREAM SEQUENCE ONE:

I'm in the dining room of some fancy country club dressed in jeans, boots, and a leather jacket. A man has stopped me. He is wearing what looks like a Norman Hilton suit, accented by a Robert Talbot regimental-stripe tie. I don't know what he has just said in the dream, but he has that look on his face. I think he told me that I don't belong in a place like this and will have to leave. The next thing I know, I have delivered a perfectly executed head-butt, which repositions his nose to the left side of his face. Blood gushes onto the front of his suit.

Startled awake by the force of the dream blow, I looked out the window at the sprawling industrial encroachment of some mid-American city, moving rapidly past. I'd been sleeping for the past several hours in the passenger seat of my friend Byron's Yukon. I could tell that Byron had locked the homing beam onto our Chicago destination, so I drifted back to sleep and didn't enter a conscious state again until we pulled into the truck stop.

The truck stop sat on Interstate 55, just south of Chicago. The morning sun reflected off the hood of the Yukon as it pulled into the parking lot and headed out to the edge of the apron, away from traffic and curiosity. Behind the Yukon, a trailer carried a jet-black Harley-Davidson Road King. As the truck came to a stop, I looked across the front seat at Byron, knowing that more than anything in the world, he wished his bike was on the trailer with mine. It takes one heck of a friend to drive a thousand miles pulling a buddy's bike, just to turn around and drive another thousand miles home. Byron had been a friend to me through thick and thin, and to be honest, the last five years had been pretty thin.

After fifteen hours on the road, we had said about all there was to say. Without a word we opened the doors of the Yukon. Byron moved around back to begin downloading the Harley. I stretched and looked south, squinting to deflect the harshness of the morning sun. For the next few days I would be heading in that direction. Then it was due west for the rest of the trip. Gazing up at the few wisps of cloud drifting across the sky, I decided it was a pretty fair morning to be heading out on the road.

"How about a hand here?" Byron was struggling to download the bike by himself. It's usually a two-man job, but Harley guys always think they can handle it alone. Byron had gotten a bit out of balance, and even his substantial girth couldn't keep the seven hundred pounds of American iron under control. I hurried around to the other side of the bike and pushed it back into balance. Byron finessed it the rest of the way down the ramp.

"Thanks," he said.

"No. Thank you." He knew what I meant. In some friendships, there's an unspoken language. "I wish you were coming along," I said — but without the same sincerity.

"No you don't." He said it with no hint of resentment. We had covered a lot of miles together over the years, but we both knew this was one trip I needed to take alone.

We gave each other a hug, and he was off. I watched the Yukon pull out of the station and then climbed onto my bike and flipped the ignition switch to the "on" position. I made sure I was in neutral. Since Illinois has no helmet laws for adults over twenty-one, I strapped my helmet on top of my saddlebags and turned my ball cap backwards.

The use of a helmet was something Elizabeth and I always argued about. It was actually one of the few things we argued about in our marriage. My argument was that a helmet tended to restrict your vision, thereby making it more likely that you might have an accident. Hers was the more logical — that if you take a baseball bat and hit a head covered by a helmet, and then take the helmet off and hit the head again, the head in the helmet always comes out in better shape.

I moved my thumb to the starter switch. There is a moment of anticipation that has always accompanied the starting of my motorcycle. It is just an instant — a moment of recognition that the ride is about to begin. I gave the starter button a push, and the big twin fired up with its signature rumble. I felt the smile spread across my face. I adjusted my sunglasses. My left foot tapped the shifter into first, and with a twist of the throttle I was on the road once again.

I headed for the on-ramp of Interstate 55. As I accelerated down the ramp I could feel the power of the Harley pushing me back, making me hang on to the handlebars to counteract the laws of physics. My smile broadened. The feel of the air hitting my face evoked all manner of memories. The rumble of the bike, the pull of my arm muscles against the thrust, the smell of pure air rushing to my head, and the energy building inside me, all combined to create that special experience that can only be achieved by hitting the road on a motorcycle. I felt it all.

The speedometer read seventy by the time I left the ramp and merged onto the interstate. Riding on interstate highway is not my first preference. It serves the purpose it was designed for — getting from point A to point B with the greatest efficiency. In typical American fashion, the destination is all, not the journey itself. My consolation was knowing that in little more than two hours all would change. When I hit Bloomington, I would switch to old Route 66. That historic highway would serve as the unifying thread guiding my trip.

It has been called the Mother Road. Winding from Chicago to Los Angeles, Route 66 has become a symbol of a better time in America. I was only a kid when Buzz and Todd cruised it every week in those pristine Corvette roadsters. It seems to me that I recall Kesey and his Merry Pranksters spending some time on it. Even Fonda and Hopper rode the highway through parts of California, Arizona, and New Mexico before heading south to New Orleans.

I chose to ride Route 66 because it gave my trip some shape — some cohesion — and because the first stop on my agenda was the home of Dr. Julius Leppick. Leppick had retired to Funk's Grove, a small town a few miles south of Bloomington, after years of prominence at the University of Chicago's Divinity School. I'd never met the man, but he was legendary in theological circles. I'd read everything he had published, and his work had motivated me to make his home my first stop. The fact that he lived just off Route 66 had given me the idea for the spatial component of the journey.

It hadn't dawned on me until later how much the old road ran through my history like some unseen stream flowing throughout the disjointed pieces of my life. I was born just off Route 66 in St. Louis, Missouri. Elizabeth was also born just off the highway, but a thousand miles away in Albuquerque, New Mexico. At least one of my children now lived on Route 66. Against all logic, I hoped that, traveling this nostalgic old stretch of road, I might find a few clues to untangle the mess I had made of my life.

❀

The ride to Bloomington was uneventful. Interstate travel usually is, unless you happen to be riding through a thunderstorm and get passed by a convoy of eighteen-wheelers. My first venture back into motorcycling came over a decade ago, when I took a cross-country trip with a few friends. The plan was simple: fly to Milwaukee, pick up a new Harley, ride back to Colorado. After an uneventful flight to Milwaukee, good service at House of Harley, and a pleasant ride to Madison, we awoke the next morning to the sound of thunder. Looking out the window of our motel, I realized things had just become a bit more complicated. Of course, being the seasoned travelers we were, what was a little rain?

An hour out of Madison, the sky opened up and the deluge began. That was when I discovered what happens when an eighteen-wheeler passes you in a thunderstorm when you do not have adequate rain gear. In seconds I was soaked and freezing. I was wearing stylish little driving gloves that gave no protection from the rain. They were soaked so thoroughly that when I finally was able to peel them off, they stuck to my hands as if they had been glued on. My boots were not much better; they almost instantly became completely drenched. The spray from the truck covered the shield of my helmet (I wore one in those days) and blinded me. The force of the draft created by the huge truck pushed and pulled me till I felt like the metal ball bouncing back and forth between the flippers of a pinball machine.

I remember the two thoughts that raced through my mind in that moment. The first was, *I'm going to die.* The second was that I should have been in Denver playing golf instead of risking my life on a motorcycle in the middle of Wisconsin. By the time I was able to pull over and get inside a rest stop, I was so tense that my shoulder muscles had turned into knots the size of small plums.

Over time, I learned when to stop and when to ride in a storm. Fortunately, this day looked as if it would stay sunny and pleasant. I cruised into Bloomington in a little under two hours and found the turnoff marked for historic Route 66 and Funk's Grove. Immediately the trip was transformed from interstate survival to back-road adventure.

❀

Riding the old road was a bit like taking a trip in a time machine. Close to the interstate, the landscape had suffered the same consequences the nearby inhabitants of such construction projects suffer. It was noisy, ugly, dirty, and functionally modern. Sterile warehouses and cookie-cutter fast-food restaurants lined the road. As the interstate faded into the background, the countryside began to move back in time. Long winding stretches of pastoral scenery replaced the concrete chaos. Trees lined the road. Small farms speckled the terrain. I arrived in Funk's Grove just about lunchtime.

Funk's Grove looked like a set from a Tennessee Williams play. It is a marvel that towns like this still exist. The road into town changed into a brick-paved street lined with huge oaks whose branches spread above the street, creating a canopy of leaves that here and there allowed the rays of the sun to penetrate to the pavement. I rode past the small city park and waved back at the children waving to me from the playground. I passed numerous signs advertising famous "Funk's Grove Pure Maple Syrup." One group of citizens stopped and stared as if they hadn't seen a motorcycle in years. Some waved. A few frowned. I passed the old Funk's Grove Country Store with its solitary Mobil gas pump out front and turned onto Elm Street.

Leppick's home was pretty close to what I had imagined. Small and quaint — professorial. The exterior of the white cottage was meticulously maintained, right down to the flowerbeds surrounding the wraparound porch. Green shutters and a gray slate roof finished off the look. I pulled into the driveway and shut down the Harley. The professor must have heard me coming. He was on the porch before I'd even climbed off the motorcycle.

"Nice bike," he said.

"Thanks."

Leppick looked about like I'd pictured in my mind. Having seen photos, his face was familiar but aged. He wore a plain gray cardigan over a white dress shirt, unbuttoned at the collar. His black, pin-striped trousers were the obvious lower half of a suit. I could imagine him having just returned from a lecture and taking off his tie and jacket, then slipping into his cardigan — a kind of academic Mr. Rogers.

"Looks like an old FL, but it must be newer," Leppick observed as he took in every square inch of the Harley — and me.

"It's actually a '98. They call it a Road King Classic. It was designed to have the old FL look but with modern technology."

"As if any Harley had 'modern technology,'" Leppick said with a wry grin.

The old boy was sharp as a tack for eighty-nine.

He stepped down off the porch and extended his hand. "Julius Leppick."

"John Calvin," I said, as I shook his hand.

"Won't you come in?"

❀

As we walked through the door, my first impression was of how the interior of the house complimented the exterior. A wall of bookshelves stood across the room from the front door, filled with leather-bound books that seemed to shout out their intellectual substance. No paperbacks here! Antique furniture filled the house just to the point of clutter. Years before, I had visited the Kilns at Oxford, where C. S. Lewis had lived. Leppick's house felt a bit like an American counterpart of the Kilns. There were oriental rugs positioned throughout the living room, covering hardwood floors. A small desk sat by the front window, much as Lewis's had at the Kilns.

"You'll have to excuse the mess," he apologized. "Since my wife passed away, my only source of cosmos in the chaos is a housekeeper who comes once a week, and unfortunately, that was five days ago."

"You wouldn't feel the need to say a word if you could see my place," I replied. "I don't even have the once-a-week reprieve from my chaos."

"Your letter made it sound like the internal clutter might be more distressing than the external," Leppick said, cutting right to the chase.

I thought for a second of how to respond. "I guess that's why I'm here," I replied.

"Sit down. Would you like some tea or coffee?" the professor offered.

"I'd love a soft drink, with a lot of ice, if you have it."

"I'm a borderline cola addict myself," he replied. "I always keep a few liters around."

"That would be great!"

As he walked into the small kitchen off the living area, I took in the rich atmosphere of the room. Were any of my books on the shelves? Probably not. One entire section of the far wall was filled with the works Leppick had produced during his illustrious career.

In his prime, Professor Leppick had seemed to defy categorization. There are two primary camps in theological circles: your theological conservatives and your theological liberals. Leppick didn't fit either group. His deep convictions concerning the inspiration of the Bible and its revelatory authority put him outside the liberal camp of most of his contemporaries at Chicago. His criticism of the bibliolatry of the fundamentalist and evangelical communities and his critique of the lack of social compassion within these groups had made him anathema within more conservative circles. He was right in the middle somewhere — the place I had once hoped to be.

The professor returned with two tall, ice-filled glasses of Coke. "It sounds like you've had a rough go of it lately," he said.

"Self-inflicted, I'm afraid," I replied.

"After I received your letter I picked up several of your books. They are quite well done."

I wasn't sure if he was serious or just being polite. "I wrote them before things came unraveled. I'm not sure how good they were. Certainly not of the academic or literary quality of your work."

We sat down in two matching overstuffed chairs, facing each other.

"I wasn't fishing for a compliment, but thank you. Actually, my work is rather obscure. It seems only the academic types can wade through it. Yours is accessible. I'm sure they have been quite helpful to many."

"I hope so, although it makes my current state all the more ironic."

"Sometimes, the journey is complex." He said it with a great deal of compassion — as well as a sense of authority that made me feel like he knew of what he spoke. "If I have one complaint against the contemporary religious environment in America, it is this: They have taken the mystery out of the mysterious. They have boxed God. Everything fits in neat little compartments. There are simple formulas for every situation. Not at all like Abraham leaving Ur and heading off to a place he knew not, I fear."

"I wrote some of those formulas, you know."

"I'd like to see what you would write now."

"I'm afraid I have nothing to offer at the moment."

"Oh, I think you probably do. Unfortunately, no one would publish it," he said with his good-natured grin.

We shot the breeze for a while before he said, "Do you mind if I ask you a question? What did you think coming here might accomplish?"

Good question. "I'm not sure. I have always respected your work, and I thought you might have some ideas about my predicament."

"In your letter you indicated that you were—how should I say it—stuck? I've tried to put myself in your situation and ask what I would do if I were you. Would I be able to make some sense out of what you have gone through? Would I know what to do next?"

He had hit the nail right on the head. He sat and thought for several minutes before continuing. "You know my own journey has been a bit unorthodox."

"Orthodoxy has not worked very well for me, I'm afraid," I said. "I'm hoping there might be something that will."

Leppick had been staring at the floor. He finally lifted his gaze and looked me in the eye. "As chaotic as your self-destructive behavior has been, I believe one day you might be able to see some purpose in all of it."

I didn't know quite how to respond. I decided to be polite. "I hope so," was all I said.

"Of course, it could go either way at this point. There is a critical point in the male spiritual journey when men must turn a corner. It often happens when a man is a little older than you are. Fifty seems to be about the norm. But occasionally, some men get ahead of schedule," he said with a smile.

"I assume you're referring to me?" I said.

"As I've studied the literature, I've come to believe that the first half of life is a time of what some call the *ascent*. These are the years when men in our culture work to make their mark." He reached down, picked up a pen from the table, and drew a simple line on his napkin, moving upward at about a forty-five degree angle. Above the line he wrote the word *ASCENT*.

"In classical spiritual formation literature, somewhere in midlife, the line is supposed to change direction. The second half of the journey is to be a time of downward movement." From near where the first line ended, he drew a second headed downward at a forty-five degree angle, then wrote the word *DESCENT* over this segment of the line. "This is what some have called the Wisdom Journey." He wrote those words under the line.

"How does this fit with my situation?" I asked.

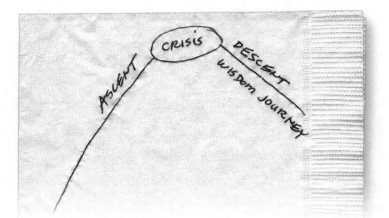

"My guess is that it doesn't, as I've drawn it. I don't see you in ascent, and I don't really see you moving into descent either. It would be hard to without a map to guide you," he explained.

"I'm still not sure I understand," I said.

"Well, right here at the top," and he pointed to the spot where the two lines almost intersected, "there is an event that occurs in many men's lives." Now he drew an oval around the point of intersection. "It usually is some kind of crisis," he said as he wrote the word *CRISIS* in the circle. "My hunch would be that you are somewhere in that circle."

I looked at the simple diagram. I looked long and hard at the word *CRISIS*. "If that's the case, what comes next?" I asked.

"I don't know," Leppick replied. "That will be between you and God."

"That is a problem."

"I'm sure," he said as he looked intensely into my eyes. "You must move toward the transcendent again," he gently suggested.

"I'm not sure I can do that."

"My fear is that if you do not make that breakthrough, you might have a nice trip on your motorbike, but you won't put your life back together again," he said.

"With all due respect, sir, I don't have the foggiest idea of how I would go about such a thing anymore," I said.

"I don't really know what it will mean for you, but I can offer a suggestion." He rose from the chair and walked to the bookcase. Looking through his books, he continued. "In my own life, the classics of spirituality helped immensely. I was steeped in Reformation theology and contemporary approaches to spirituality. I lived in the arrogance of the time that seemed to think that nothing of value had been written prior to the previous decade. When I began my own quest for authenticity, I went back to the classics. We have two thousand years of history in the Church, you know. I found a depth and reality in the early writers that created a hunger for what they had. It changed the course of my life. I stayed at Chicago, but nothing was ever the same."

He pulled a small book from the shelf and turned back toward me. "Obviously, I can't send my entire library with you," he said. "I'll get you started and send you to a dear friend who has also made some progress on the downward journey. Have you read *The Way of a Pilgrim*?"

"No." Ironically, I had quoted from the book in one of my pieces but had never actually read the original.

"It's an older version of your motorcycle trip, written in Russia about three hundred years ago. Traditionally, authorship is attributed to a simple Russian peasant, but personally, without doing the critical work, I've always believed the pilgrim must have been someone like myself, an academic, wishing he could escape the confines of the cloister and head out on the road. This pilgrim did not enjoy the luxury of a motorized vehicle. He walked. Like yourself, he too had lost everything, although not of his own doing.

"One day, the peasant walked into a church where the priest was speaking on the text, 'Pray without ceasing.' The pilgrim began to long to know how he could achieve this state of constant spiritual connection. He asked the priest who'd given the message — only to find that, although the priest could give a message on the subject, he had no idea how to actually do it. I always laugh when I think about this encounter. It seems far too familiar for comfort. I guess nothing is new under the sun.

"The pilgrim set out to discover how to pray in this manner. The book is the story of his journey." The professor handed me a well-read version of the text, bound in leather.

I held the book in my hands. It was obviously very old. It had to be worth a great deal. "I can't take this," I said.

"I insist. It won't be long before all these books will be placed in some obscure corner of the University of Chicago's library. I doubt anyone would even check it out. I don't have any family left. My wife and I were never able to have children. It would give me a great deal of pleasure if you took it and read it on your trip. I think you will find it helpful. I would ask only two things of you."

"Anything," I replied.

"First, begin to do what the pilgrim did."

"Which is?"

"Not to take away from your enjoyment of the book's unfolding story, but let me ask you a question. How is your prayer experience?"

"It's been nonexistent for the last five years," I said.

"Then I'm going to ask you to begin to pray again."

"I'd love to, but it just doesn't work for me anymore."

"I suggest that very thought is part of what has you feeling so conflicted."

"I can't help it. There is absolutely no sense of reality in prayer for me. It seems so futile," I said.

"I'm going to ask you to take the spiritual direction of an old man. It is all I'm going to ask. Could you not indulge me for the few days of your trip?"

"I'm willing to try," I conceded, with little enthusiasm.

"Good. Now I'm going to tell you something about prayer that will go against everything you ever learned in seminary or wrote about in your books. I do seem to recall you actually wrote about prayer," Leppick shot at me with a twinkle in his eye.

"Don't rub salt in the wound."

"Sorry, sometimes I can't help myself. I'm just an old man."

"Right!"

"In the book, the pilgrim comes to a hermitage where a monk gives him instructions for learning what he calls perpetual, interior prayer. This is what the book is most famous for, although I've discovered that most of those from conservative circles who read the book can't seem to see beyond the trees to perceive the forest. The pilgrim is taught the Jesus Prayer: 'Lord Jesus Christ, have mercy on me.'"

"I first encountered it in J. D. Salinger," I said.

"*Franny and Zoe.* An unfortunate distortion," Leppick replied. "Here is what I am going to ask. I want you to begin to pray the Jesus Prayer as you ride down the road. Every time you think of it, I want you to say out loud or even sub-vocally, 'Lord Jesus Christ, have mercy on me.'"

I thought for a moment and then reluctantly said, "I'll do it. But I have to warn you; it won't mean anything to me."

"This is where I am going to tell you something that you've probably never been told: It doesn't matter."

It was late afternoon when I left the professor and rolled out of Funk's Grove, heading south. The day was magnificent. The trees had begun to change their colors as fall approached. The temperature was at that perfect point where you don't feel either hot or cold. I passed few cars heading in either direction. The Harley just kept rumbling along, and the sound of the bike on the old pavement had an almost hypnotic effect. I slowed the bike to just under fifty and began taking in the sights of the rural countryside.

When I got to McLean, I stopped for a piece of pie and a cup of coffee at the Dixie Trucker's Home. Springfield, only an hour away, was about as far as I wanted to ride on my first day on the road.

My second promise to Leppick had been to stop in St. Louis and visit a friend of his. I had some business of my own in St. Louis, but a good night's rest was at the top of my agenda.

✸

I took Business 55 into the heart of Springfield and began to look for a cafe and a hotel with a bit of character. The Springfield Hotel fit the bill. It sat on old Main Street and came complete with a sign in the window that said, "Lincoln Slept Here." I pulled up to the curb and looked at the red brick structure. It looked old enough — maybe he really had.

After locking my bike, I pulled the bag liners out of the saddlebags and headed into the hotel. The old check-in desk looked as if it could have been the original. The young woman behind the desk had a cheery countenance and welcomed me warmly. "Can I help you?"

"I could use a room for the night and a suggestion for a great place to eat," I said.

"I think I can take care of both."

I signed the register and dropped my bags in the room before heading out to the Thunderbird Bar and Grill. "Not only is the food great," I'd been assured by the check-in clerk, "but they have one of the best country-western bands in Illinois. A lot of guys like you hang out there."

When I pulled up to the restaurant and saw the row of shiny motorcycles parked out front, I guessed my mode of transportation had revealed just what kind of a guy she thought I was. I backed the Harley into a spot just vacated by a previous patron.

It was a good tip. The band was good — really good. The place was packed, and the energy was high. The crowd contained an interesting mix of people. I could pick out the guys who came on bikes by the relatively new, obviously expensive leathers they wore. Most of them seemed like young professionals who rode not as a way of life but as a means of mental health. My kind of guys. Most of them were dancing with attractive women. In this sense, they weren't at all like me.

❀

"What can I get you, friend?"

I looked up and immediately knew I was in trouble. She had red hair. "Something to help a fellow make it a little farther down the road," I replied, unable to take my eyes off her. She wasn't stunning — but definitely cute. I guessed she must have been in her early to mid-thirties. Her look perfectly fit the ambiance of the place, and I figured she must have had about a dozen guys a night hitting on her. I resolved that I would not be one.

"Well, that can mean a lot of things," she countered with a friendly smile. "Would you like a drink or something to eat?"

"I better have both. What's the house specialty?"

"Our steaks are the best east of the Mississippi," she offered. "Of course the real specialty of the house is the world's greatest waitresses."

"I can see that," I said. "I'll have a T-bone, medium rare, and as cold a bottle of Rolling Rock as you can dig up."

She walked away writing down the order, and I admired the view. Lord have mercy! Was that the prayer? Tight 501's and wavy, red hair — Beatrice in blue jeans!

I tried to think about the coming days in St. Louis as I ate, although it was hard to keep my mind focused with Jeannie, my siren/waitress, frequently checking on me. I couldn't help noticing that a few guys at the bar were starting to take more than a bit of interest in her, too. Jeannie was obviously bugged, but she handled them with style. When she brought me a fresh Rolling Rock, I asked what was going on.

"Those guys?" she responded. "They hang out here trying to imagine they have a life."

"Are they bothering you?" I asked.

"Yeah, but I can handle it. I'm used to their type."

I was hoping I didn't fall into the category. "I'll tell them to back off if you'd like," I said.

"Don't worry, I'll be fine," she said. "You're not from around here, are you?"

"Nope. I'm on a trip across country on old Route 66."

"Sounds like fun," she said.

"Fun and a bit of nostalgia to clear the old gray matter."

"You aren't the first to make that trip."

"No doubt," I said.

Jeannie turned and walked back toward the bar.

I don't quite remember all that happened next. One of the creeps must have grabbed her as she walked past. I heard the crash of the tray and turned in time to see her slap his face. When he grabbed her arm, I was out of my chair and in his face before I had time to think. "Hands off, buddy."

His response was a direct quote from Nixon's White House tapes.

The bartender was there in an instant.

"Take it easy, boys," he said. "If you need to settle this, take it outside."

"Yeah, outside," he challenged, this time calling me a name I quit using sometime shortly after junior high.

"With pleasure."

I could see the mix of fear and anger in Jeannie's eyes. I also knew I probably should have tried a more diplomatic approach. The bartender was on the phone, so I figured that if I could delay the fight long enough, the police might spare this jerk some pain and me some trouble I didn't need.

Unfortunately, no sooner were we outside than Mr. Wonderful reached to pull out what appeared to be about a seven-inch blade. I knew what I had to do, although in the present circumstance it was a bit risky. My dad had taught me that the best way to handle a bully is to hit him in the nose as hard as you can before he has a chance to hit you. Before the knife was out of the scabbard I had connected so thoroughly with my new friend's nose that blood flew from it like an open fire hydrant on a hot day. I knew that if you follow dad's advice well, you also make it nearly impossible for the bully to see. Then I added my own bully-defeating move to the one dad taught me. While he was grabbing his nose and screaming, I kicked him as hard as I could right between the legs with my motorcycle boot. This all took his friend by such surprise that he just stood dumbfounded, like a deer caught in the headlights.

By now a small crowd was pouring out of the restaurant. I could hear the sound of a siren in the distance and knew that if I didn't get out of there, pronto, I would have to go into a lot of explanations I really didn't want to make in front of a bunch of strangers — and Jeannie.

"Think I'll get out of here," I told her.

"I'm coming with you," she said.

I forced myself to say, "I don't think that would be a good idea."

"No, I'm serious. I've had all I can take for one night, and I could use a little motorcycle ride."

"I'm staying clear down at the Springfield Hotel," I said.

"Perfect," she said.

***

We sat in the coffee shop of the Springfield Hotel and talked till after midnight, trading war stories. She had not had good luck with men.

"Now tell me something about yourself," she said. "I've virtually spilled my guts to you."

"Okay," I said. "I'll tell you why I have chosen a self-imposed vow of celibacy."

I could tell she was not ready for that piece of info. "Celibacy?" she said.

"Let me tell you the story," I said. "My wife and I split up a few years back. I had some serious problems, and we couldn't keep the marriage together." I wasn't being totally honest, but I didn't want to explain all the lurid details, either. "I had this friend, Rick, and he had a wife. Her name was Kelly."

I wasn't sure how much I was going to tell her about this. It was part of a complicated set of relationships with women that spanned the last few years. Testosterone gets a lot of guys into a lot of trouble. In fact, a couple of years after my divorce, I actually went to see a doctor to find out if some excess of testosterone was causing the intensity of my sexual drive. The doctor assured me that nothing was physically abnormal and suggested that I might want to see a psychologist. I had to laugh. My parole had been conditioned upon extensive therapy, and I would have agreed to anything to stay out of jail. So I'd already had two years of intensive therapy, and I was sure that whatever was going on with my sex life was more likely the result of seeing a shrink than something that could be solved by one. That's when I'd decided to become temporarily celibate.

"Kelly had the kind of lips that seemed to call out, 'Kiss me,'" I said. "You know the kind. Kim Basinger, Angelina Jolie, Michelle Pfieffer, Angie Edgerton."

"Who is Angie Edgerton?" she interrupted.

"I was seeing her before the disaster with Kelly," I said.

"Oh . . ."

"There was also Sydna. She was before Angie."

"Oh," she said again.

"And Francie . . . and a few others." This time she didn't say anything. I decided it would be best to get back to the story.

"Along with the lips, Kelly had the whole package: great figure, sultry face, and blonde hair that fell to her shoulders. You get the idea."

Jeannie remained quiet. She was probably trying to figure out what to do with the list of women I had just fired off in light of my celibacy announcement.

"She and Rick had just called it quits after a brief and disastrous marriage. I made the mistake of thinking we could just be friends.

"At first, we commiserated together. I'd been divorced for a year, but there was still hope for the marriage. My wife was willing to try to work things out. Rick still loved Kelly, but they were like oil and water when they were together. Kelly had been devastated by the divorce. She and I had been friends for years, so spending time together seemed innocent enough. I should have known better. When emotions are scrambled, the mind thinks strange thoughts and the hormones rage. I think it was Viktor Frankl who observed that the sexual libido runs rampant in the existential vacuum."

Jeannie didn't seem to quite get the reference.

"She showed up at my door one evening wearing a dress that communicated a whole lot more than friendship. My feelings had been changing from friendship to desire, and that dress reinforced my hunch that maybe she was feeling the same.

"I fixed pasta and salad, and we drank a lot of wine. After dinner we moved to the sofa and sat in front of the fireplace. It was way too romantic for a couple of friends. My heart was pounding, and my hands were sweating. I felt like a junior-high kid on his first date. I put my arm around her and pulled her to me. She didn't resist. I kissed her. She kissed me. The passion produced by our mutual pain was nearly uncontrollable. We didn't leave the loft for three days. We actually thought it was love — at least for the first few weeks."

"What happened?" Jeannie finally said.

"The biochemistry of romantic love is another good reason to question the entire evolutionary theory," I said. "The human brain just sits there indiscriminately producing phenylethylamine, and we suddenly find ourselves 'falling in love.' Behavior that prior to this experience would have seemed insane now seems perfectly normal. The feelings produced by this process will carry a relationship anywhere from a few weeks to a few years, but at some point, reality comes crashing in. For Kelly and me, it took almost a month. By then, both Rick and Elizabeth had found out about the affair, and both had placed the blame on me. The damage that did to my relationship with Elizabeth — and the destruction of my friendship with Rick — just about rounded out the complete annihilation of my previous life.

"One morning I woke up and looked at Kelly sleeping next to me and realized that I really did care for her. Unfortunately, or fortunately, depending on how you look at it, I cared for her like a sister. We called it quits on Valentine's Day. I haven't been with a woman since. Temporary, self-imposed celibacy, voila!"

Jeannie responded as had other women since I'd decided to refrain from physical intimacy — she seemed to be relieved to spend the evening with a man without sex being the primary agenda. We continued to talk about our lives for the next few hours. I have no idea what time it was when we decided to head up to my room. Jeannie slept on the bed. I slept on the floor. We had breakfast together at the Lincoln Café, and I was on the road by ten.

Missouri

Journal — September 12: *Who is this woman in my bed? Not a great start for a spiritual journey. I'm not sure what I think about Leppick's theory. I certainly have attempted the ascent part of the journey. Upward mobility — the American way of life. As for the downward journey, I'm not sure I buy it. I certainly haven't seen a great deal of emphasis on "descent" in the circles I run in. The crisis part — that, I can relate to! Somehow, I was never taught any of this. I should have learned it in St. Louis.*

⊛

The sky was overcast as I rolled out of Springfield. I had only been on the road about fifteen minutes when the heavens opened, and the rain came down hard. When I first started riding a motorcycle, I hated days like this. Over time, I learned that good rain gear, a windshield, and a pair of goggles can make riding in the rain a surprisingly pleasant experience. I stopped under the first overpass I came to and put on my rain gear. The Harley had a great windshield, and I pulled a pair of goggles out of my saddlebags. Thus prepared, I started the bike and waited for a break in traffic to get back on the road. The woman riding shotgun in the first car that passed looked out the window at me and shook her head with disgust. Obviously not a cycling aficionado. I was only sixty miles from St. Louis, and because of the weather conditions, I was actually grateful for the Interstate.

When I got into the St. Louis area, I swung around the outer belt of the Interstate to pick up Route 66 again. There were a few classic spots on the old road that I wanted to see, and I'd already decided to spend a night at the Coral Court Motel.

Sitting a mile southwest of the St. Louis city limits, the motel is a slice right out of the glory days of Route 66. Built in 1941, the place is pure Art Deco. The rounded exterior walls were made of that yellow brick so popular in the fifties. The windows were made of opaque glass blocks. The whole look was topped off with a southwestern red tile roof. Think streamline deco architecture at its hideous best. In its heyday, every room at the place was booked weeks in advance. The fact that each room had its own garage made it especially appealing for the safety of the

Harley. I checked in and decided to wait for the weather to break before heading into the heart of St. Louis. When I hit the room, I collapsed onto the bed and was out in minutes.

❁

I hadn't been to St. Louis for nearly thirty years. In theory, this was my home. I was born here. I lived here during the first five years of my life, supposedly the most formative. I believe it. My most vivid memory of childhood is of standing alone in the driveway of our family home. In my mind's eye, I see a lonely and sad little boy. Even now, in my forties, I can still feel his sadness. It makes me want to go stand in the driveway of the Coral Court in the rain.

My family left St. Louis when I was five. The extended family had lived here for four generations. Great-Great Grandfather Schilling was part of that mass of German immigrants who came to America from Württemberg in the middle of the nineteenth century. St. Louis was one of their major destinations. The heritage lives on in the monster breweries that helped put the city on the map. After the Civil War, John Schilling's son Benjamin became the owner and operator of the Four-Mile House saloon. His daughter Henrietta was my grandmother. No one in the family ever talked about roots. I have a feeling they weren't all that wonderful. I also have the sense that most immigrants from that era wanted to forget the life they'd left behind, while their grandchildren search to rediscover it.

Grandma married Augustus Meiusi. Grandpa was a first generation immigrant from Estonia. He'd stowed away on a ship sailing out of Riga, Latvia, in 1910. When the ship landed in Florida, he jumped. I come from good illegal-alien stock. From Florida, he worked his way to St. Louis. There he met my grandmother. Why Augustus and Henrietta married remains a mystery. Of course, why anyone marries is something of a mystery. Henrietta was chubby and plain. Augustus was handsome and athletic. I have this hunch he cut a deal with Benjamin Schilling, who just happened to be a customer on his pickle route. Augustus and Etta ended up in the restaurant business and had one child—a daughter, my mother.

Grandma was the center of human warmth in our family. All my positive childhood memories are filled with her. Grandpa was one mean dude. We lived next door to them—3310 Carson Road, home of the emotional Addams family.

❀

DREAM SEQUENCE TWO:

I'm in the backyard of Stevie Phillips's house. I'm supposed to meet my friend, Hank, who has a set of keys for an old Honda I'm going to borrow. Something is wrong with my Harley. I don't want to ride the Honda, but I need to get somewhere. The Honda is sitting in Stevie's yard when Hank's wife, Rita, arrives, wearing a silver, metallic bikini. She tells me the keys to the bike are in her purse in the guesthouse in Stevie's backyard. I follow her into the guesthouse, taking careful notice of her well-defined legs. She reaches into her purse and pulls out the keys. She brings them to me and moves right into my personal space. Her face is an inch from mine, and the look in her eye is inviting. I know this is wrong. I know I shouldn't. I lean toward her, and she responds. We kiss. Just then a car pulls into the driveway and shines its headlights on us. I have to get to the Honda and get out of here. The glare of the lights is blinding as I grope to find the ignition. I can't get the key in the slot . . .

I came to consciousness staring at the ceiling of my Coral Court room. Dreams. Man, are they weird! How do you end up with Rita Connor wearing a metal bikini in Stevie Phillips's backyard?

I was sure that careful analysis of the dream would provide more insight into my twisted psyche, but at the moment I was more aware of the Jesus Prayer than the dream. I hadn't done a good job of honoring my commitment to Leppick.

I pulled *The Way of a Pilgrim* from my saddlebag and started to read.

By the grace of God I am a Christian, by my deeds a great sinner, and by my calling a homeless wanderer of humblest origin, roaming from place to place. My possessions consist of a knapsack with dry crusts of bread on my back and in my bosom the Holy Bible. This is all!

The writing wasn't great, but then it hadn't become a spiritual classic on the basis of its literary value. I hadn't gotten to the Jesus Prayer part yet, but I found myself reflecting on the content of the prayer. *Lord Jesus Christ.* Those are words I once embraced. As an agnostic university student, I once got into an argument with one of my classmates on the subject of religion. I remembered it vividly. We were drinking green beer on St. Patrick's Day at Kelly's bar in Kansas City. At the time, I was a senior at the university, studying philosophy. By this point in my academic career, I had examined nearly every other popular belief system in vogue at the end of that infamous decade of the sixties. I was pretty sure that Christianity would prove as harmless as the rest.

My classmate challenged me to read C. S. Lewis's *Mere Christianity*. This was in my pseudo-intellectual phase, and the thought that an Oxford professor had been an apologist for a religious system intrigued me. I was sure no educated twentieth-century man would actually buy into the myth that an itinerant Jewish carpenter could walk on water.

My examination became an obsession. By the end of the year, I had become convinced of the historicity of the person and baffled by the magnitude of the claims of Jesus. The evidence on behalf of the resurrection seemed compelling. Lewis himself made reference to being the most reluctant convert in all of England and being brought "kicking and struggling" into the faith by the sheer weight of the evidence.

The final "nudge" in my life had been a somewhat mystical experience of certitude that came while reading the gospel of John. It was a minor epiphany, but one that sustained me for years. I intellectually and emotionally embraced the Christian faith.

It seemed like a faint memory now. It wasn't that I had come to doubt the actual truth of the person of Christ. I just couldn't live under the cultural captivity of Jesus that had shaped Christianity in America. Had I been able to, I certainly would not have been spending the night at the Coral Court.

Have mercy on me. Now, *this* part of the prayer I could relate to. It was my only hope. I had fallen from grace; I needed mercy. I couldn't see how saying this part of the prayer could hurt someone like me, and it just might help.

I looked out the window. The rain had let up. I decided to get about my business.

Leppick's friend was Joseph Monroe. Like Leppick, he held a PhD and had been a full professor. Unlike Leppick, Monroe taught English literature at Washington University, one of the finest private schools in America. Monroe had been one of its giants. Retired for nearly ten years, he was, like Leppick, a widower living by himself. Of course, St. Louis isn't quite Funk's Grove.

Monroe still lived in the university area. I rode northeast up Watson Road till it intersected Brentwood Boulevard. Traffic was relatively heavy, and riding a motorcycle through urban traffic takes all the concentration you can muster. I was conscious of the guy in the red Jeep Wrangler immediately in front of me, who was spending way too much time looking at his girlfriend, and the silver Honda coming up from behind that appeared to have a teenager with a cell phone behind the wheel. I also watched upcoming side streets, trying to determine if the drivers behind the wheels of the cars at each stop looked as if they might enjoy pulling out in front of a motorcycle and thereby launching the rider into the wild blue yonder like a clown shot out of a cannon.

Brentwood Boulevard ran into the inner belt that took me past the high-rent district of Clayton. I felt compelled to pull off and cruise Clayton Road. Instead of the small ranch-style homes in the Coral Court section of town, Clayton was filled with block after block of homes that looked more like hotels than personal residences.

This was the suburb in which Clayton Presbyterian Church was located. I had been approached about the senior pastor position at the church in the days when I had ecclesiastical ambitions. At the time, I thought a return to St. Louis might help me reconnect with my roots. Of course, my roots were not of the Clayton ilk. The pulpit committee decided I didn't fit the milieu of the congregation — obviously a good decision on their part, given what happened to me in the following years. It also was probably a good thing for me, considering that their next pastor committed suicide.

I stayed on Clayton Road until it intersected Hanley Road. No more mansions here! Instead, smaller houses with smaller yards. Most were neat, clean bungalows that looked as if they had been acquired by young professionals who delighted in renovating these modest homes. Young collegians and retired people strolled the sidewalks on this pleasant evening. I passed a coffee shop where the outdoor patio contained a sprinkling of the young and upwardly mobile. This was obviously one of the up-and-coming areas in St. Louis.

My presence in the neighborhood was attracting a great deal of attention. Adults stopped and stared as I rode by, while children waved or gave me the thumbs up. The sound of the modified exhaust on the Harley often had that effect.

Monroe lived just off the intersection of Hanley and Delmar Boulevard in a modest brick bungalow. A covered porch ran across the front of the home, much like my family's old house on Carson Road. Monroe's was larger, but the look was definitely the same. A scholarly looking, white-haired gentleman was sitting on a glider on the porch. He waved as I pulled into the driveway.

"Leppick told me you had a beautiful bike!" he exclaimed from the porch.

"Thanks," I replied, not yet knowing what to make of Monroe. He could have passed for Einstein's long-lost brother with his flowing, white hair and monstrous handlebar mustache. He was wearing baggy, khaki pants that had seen better days and a pair of black Converse high-tops that looked as if he had been wearing them since the Second World War. In bold letters his sweatshirt commanded, "READ, YOU FOOL!"

The neighborhood kids were already beginning to gather around the Harley as I put down the kickstand.

"Grab your things, and come on up. If you leave anything out there these Munchkins are bound to rip it off," he said with a huge smile, directing his comments at the children more than me.

"I left everything back at my hotel, so I think I'm safe," I said.

Monroe met me at the top of the porch steps. He was a small man with a bit of a stoop to his back. After the striking resemblance to Einstein, the first characteristic that caught my attention was his eyes. They were a brilliant blue. Looking into them gave me the eerie feeling that a much younger man was somehow trapped inside this aging body.

"I don't suppose Leppick told you about our disastrous Harley adventure in the thirties?" he asked as he extended his hand.

"No. He didn't even tell me that he ever rode a motorcycle."

"Oh, he wouldn't. Too much *hubris*. We both rode the original springers back then and dreamed of riding cross-country. We made it as far as Oklahoma City," Monroe said as he shook my hand with a firm grip.

"Why no farther?" I asked

"It rained for five days straight, and the roads were a mess. They weren't all paved in those days, you know. Leppick said he had had enough. He wouldn't even ride the motorcycle back to Chicago. He sold it for a fraction of what he paid for it to the local Harley dealer and took the train. I never let him live it down. Joe Monroe, by the way, and I believe you are Dr. John Calvin," he said, finally letting go of my hand.

"It's been awhile since anyone called me that. You can just call me John."

"One of the nice things about academia—they never take your degrees away. I know some of your story, and you are still a doctor, if not a reverend. I have to confess, I've always thought the 'reverend' business was a bit presumptuous for Protestants anyway. It somehow seems contradictory to the Reformation belief in the priesthood of all believers. Anyway, you can call me Joe, plain and simple."

We sat on the porch and drank fresh lemonade while I told

him my family's St. Louis history. Finally, we got to the point.

"I'm not quite sure whether Jules sent you here for your sake or mine," Monroe said. "I fear he thinks I'm wasting away here in this urban blight while he enjoys the bliss of rural Americana there in Funk's whatever."

"I had the feeling that he felt you might have something of value to add to my journey," I said. "He was quite adamant that he would not give me his copy of *The Way of a Pilgrim* unless I swore I would see you."

"Ah, the Jesus Prayer. What do you think?" he asked, with genuine curiosity.

"I'm not sure yet," I replied. "I only started using it yesterday."

"Have you read any of the book yet?"

"Not much."

"It has some fascinating encounters," Monroe reflected. "It is quite like the twelfth-century French tale of Parzifal."

"I'm not sure I've heard that one," I confessed.

"I'm sure you have," Monroe countered. "Only you probably know it by its later title, 'The Quest for the Holy Grail.' Mallory popularized it in the fifteenth century by placing it in the context of *Le Morte d'Arthur*, but it really predates Mallory by three centuries."

"It's been awhile since I read Mallory. The Grail quest always fascinated me."

"And now you're on it!" he exclaimed.

I laughed and shook my head. "I'm just riding my bike and trying to figure a few things out. Nothing quite as heroic as the quest for the Grail, I'm afraid."

"On the contrary. The story of the Grail is mythic and archetypal. It is the relentless pursuit of that which brings peace to the center. I would say that your current pilgrimage is quite similar."

"It might take more than the Grail to put my life back together."

"On the contrary," he said, again with great zeal. I could imagine him standing in the front of a lecture hall and holding a room full of students spellbound with his passionate discourse. "It is exactly the Grail that you seek. The Grail is only an image. Tradition identifies it as the cup of Christ at the Last Supper. Other tradition has Joseph of Arimathea collecting the blood of Christ in it at the Cross. Both have it coming to England with Joseph in the first century. But the story is not only about the literal Grail, if it even ever existed. The importance of the Grail is in what it represents. It is the symbol of the presence of the Holy One. Where the Grail is, there is the Lord. It can only be found by leaving home or the Round Table, depending on the version. The longing of the heart is always what the Grail represents."

I liked Monroe. He was one of those people you would like even if you were trying not to — a genuine character.

"I don't know. It sounds pretty romantic. I'm not sure I have the capability of taking on the quest," I said.

"So you've given up?" He seemed incredulous.

"I thought I had. But it seems that I don't even have the ability to do that. I mean, here I am."

"I assume I am supposed to say something that might somehow help you," Monroe said as he looked up at the ceiling. "Have you had dinner?" he asked suddenly, as if his mind had just shifted onto another track.

"No."

"Let's go get something to eat," he said.

"We would have to take your car."

"Nonsense!" Monroe objected. "I would love a ride on the back of that marvelous machine in my driveway. Would you mind?"

"Of course not. It would be an honor."

"Let me grab a jacket and a hat."

In thirty seconds Dr. Joseph Monroe, illustrious professor of English literature, stood before me in one of the more well-worn leather bomber jackets in captivity. He wore a black beret and carried what looked like an antique pair of goggles.

"Let's boogie!" he exclaimed with a laugh.

✦

I started the Harley, and Monroe climbed on the back.

"Where to, Professor?" I asked.

"Where did you used to live?"

"3310 Carson Road. Just off Natural Bridge Road."

"Not far from U.M. St. Louis. Would you like to see your old neighborhood?"

"It's been over thirty years, but I actually had a dream about it this afternoon."

"Take a right at the corner. We'll catch something to eat up there."

We had only been on the road a few minutes when we turned onto Carson Road from St. Charles Rock Road. These were the streets of my early youth. I had actually spent another year in St. Louis when I was twelve, the year my parents divorced and my mother and I came to live with my grandparents. Riding down Carson Road triggered memories right and left. It looked exactly the same as I remembered it although I could see that the neighborhood was more ethnically mixed than when we lived here. I knew that around the next big curve we would hit the street that held many of the mysteries of my psychological development.

"Whoa!" I exclaimed, as we came around the curve where my childhood home had been.

"What is it?" asked Monroe, leaning over my shoulder.

"It's all gone!" I said in disbelief. "They made it a dang freeway!"

I pulled over at the first street to get my bearings. Carson Road wasn't exactly a freeway, but it was six lanes wide, and lane six ran directly through the spot where our house and Grandma and Grandpa's house and Randy's house and Joey Licata's house and the rest had been. They had all been torn down to widen the road.

"My childhood is gone. They paved it!"

"They call it progress," the Professor said. "I remember this street. I think I even stopped at a little neighborhood store here once on my way to the Normandy campus."

"It was over on what used to be that corner," I pointed. "I loved that little store! I'm really freaked out!"

"I can tell," Monroe empathized.

"Let's get out of here," I said as I pulled back onto the street and headed past the corner where Randy Tucker used to live. Pam Starkey. Whatever happened to Pam Starkey? How strange to think of people you hadn't thought of in thirty or forty years.

At the corner of Natural Bridge, I took a left per Monroe's instructions. "Where are we going?" I asked.

"I know just the spot. Keep heading west toward the airport. Have you eaten at a Steak-and-Shake recently?"

"We don't have them in Colorado."

Thank God for small unchanging slices of life that provide an anchor of stability in the ocean of hyper-change. Steak-and-Shake looked just the same. They still had carhops shuttling food out to the cars parked next to the little drive-in speakers, and it still appeared to be the place to be seen. The cars were new as they made their slow procession through the drive-in, and the styles of clothing on the kids had changed, but the basic restaurant was still the same. We parked the bike and went inside to eat with the old people.

The professor ordered a double cheeseburger, fries, and a strawberry shake. I wondered if he ate like this on a regular basis. I ordered a single burger and a cup of coffee.

Monroe dove into his food with his characteristic zeal. I picked at mine. I talked about the experience of seeing the old neighborhood.

"I thought seeing things might . . . I don't know, might help give me a clue about what has been going on in my life. I sometimes wonder if what's happened goes all the way back here. I've been through it a dozen times in therapy and still can't seem to get resolution. Seeing everything gone was so strange," I said.

"Could I make an observation?" Monroe asked as he attempted to wipe a huge glob of ketchup from his moustache with his already overused and crumbling paper napkin.

"Sure."

"Without sounding too presumptuous, let an old man tell you something he learned the hard way over the years."

"Go ahead."

"Whatever demons you battle, whatever has happened in the past, whatever psychological scars you might bear, and however traumatic your childhood might have been, the answers you seek are not in the past."

"What do you mean?"

"Every Carson Road gets paved. Life is like that. What you're looking for is not in the past, nor in the future. What you seek will always be in the present."

I said nothing. We quietly continued our dinner.

"What did you and Jules talk about?" he asked.

"He told me about the ups and downs of life," I said.

"I assume you mean the ascent and descent concepts?" he said.

"He gave me a brief overview and talked a bit about the crisis. Apparently, he was pretty convinced that I am somewhere in the middle of it at the moment."

Monroe seemed to ponder for a moment and then said, "Since you came here to discover something about your childhood, I'll show you another piece that fits into the model."

Like Leppick, Monroe took a napkin and drew a figure similar to the one I had in my pocket that Leppick had drawn. Monroe added a small vertical line near the beginning of the upward ascent line of the diagram, then pointed to it with his pen. "This line," he said, "is one of the most important parts of the male journey."

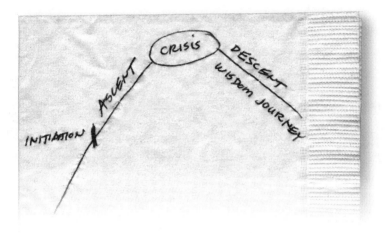

"What is it?" I asked.

"This is the point where male initiation takes place," he answered. "Without initiation, the journey gets very confusing."

"How's that?"

"In a sense, the initiation prepares you for the ascent, the crisis, and the descent. This is where a boy is taught what it means to be a man in his culture."

"What is the initiation in our culture?" I asked.

"That is the point!" he exclaimed with such gusto that I almost fell out of the booth. "We don't have one!" He continued, speaking slowly and deliberately. "Every culture in the history of human civilization seems to have had some way to initiate their young men, except for the recent West. We don't have one. The closest we have is the Jewish bar mitzvah, which has become nothing more for many Jewish families than a social requirement. How many Jewish boys do you know who act like responsible adults at age thirteen?" he asked.

"I have a group of Jewish friends I've known since I was thirteen, and they *still* don't act like responsible adults," I said.

"I've done some study on this, and the only groups in the West that do a pretty good job on this are the ultra-orthodox Jews and the Mormons."

"The Mormons?" I said, puzzled.

"Yes. The whole Mormon mission experience is a perfect model of male initiation. They indoctrinate their boys, and then they send them out of the tribe to fend for themselves in the world. When they are finished with their mission, they return to the tribe and take their place as men, not boys. Of course, they do it quite late, but in the culture of the modern West, even that makes some sense," Monroe said.

"Male initiation is supposed to impart to the young man the secrets and sacred truths of the tribe. It is the time when the young man is taken from his mother by the men of the tribe and is not returned until he has become a man. Of course, it is only the final act of many years spent imparting the cultural values to the male of the tribe."

I could tell Monroe was really into this. I wasn't sure yet what it had to do with me. "So how does this tie into the ascent and descent concepts?" I asked.

"Men are going to attempt to ascend. It is in the DNA, you might say. They are warriors by nature. They will seek power. It is a rare culture that does not exhibit this principle. Ascending is conquering. Americans do it by trying to land good jobs that pay big salaries so that they can buy big houses and fancy cars. Australian aborigines do it by going into the wilderness and fighting wild animals and waiting to have their vision quest. I think the aborigines are way ahead of us on this one.

"Eventually, men age. They reach a point where it doesn't really work to keep ascending. If they have been properly initiated, they won't be surprised or unprepared when this happens. They will know it is time to start the descent. They will know what to do with their pain."

"You lost me," I told Monroe.

"It's all about initiation. Initiation tells a boy what it means to be a man. It imparts to him the values of the tribe and sets out a roadmap for life. It teaches him how to handle his power and what to do with his pain. It sets the boy up for the crisis and the descent."

"I'm still not sure what you mean," I said.

"Okay. Let me put it another way. What are the big truths that a boy needs to know before he becomes a man?"

"I'd have to think about that one a bit," I said.

"Let me give you one possibility. I'll tell you five facts I think a boy in America needs to be taught at this point."

"Fire at will," I said.

"Life is hard," he said. "That is the first fact. Did anyone adequately teach you this truth when you were a boy?"

"I would have to say I learned it the hard way," I answered.

"You and 99 percent of the men in America." He drew a line off the initiation line and wrote, 'Life — hard!' on the napkin.

"You are going to die," he said. "That is the second big truth." He drew a second line and added, "You — die!" to the diagram.

"Try to teach that one to a sixteen-year-old! Yet, it is universally acknowledged that until we come to terms with the fact that we are going to die, we can't learn how to live. Ernest Becker postulated that the denial of death was the root of all neurosis, yet we hide death in our culture. As soon as someone dies, we have the body rushed away to the funeral home. Often it is cremated before the family even has a chance to see it. Then we have a nice sterile "memorial" service without a body. That is not how most of the world, for most of history, dealt with death."

I could see that we were being stared at by a few of the customers who didn't know what to do with Monroe's enthusiastic, "You are going to die!"

"Let's head back to your place," I suggested. "We can finish the discussion there."

All the way to his house Monroe continued to lecture in my right ear. He was on a roll!

"For most cultures, death is a part of daily life. Multiple generations live together, and the tribe shares in all the experiences of the families. Someone is always dying. But the body is not rushed away. It is placed where all can see and honor the person. It is right there, serving as a hands-on reminder that people die."

By the time we got back to his house, it was getting late — and I'd heard plenty more about the death experience. But I really wanted to know about the other three items he felt should be included in the initiation rite.

We sat down at the kitchen table. Monroe took the napkin, which was beginning to suffer a bit from the wear, and drew three more lines under the "You — die!" line. By the first he wrote, "You — not important!"

"Most of us spend our lives with the illusion that somehow we are at the center of the universe. We learn it from the moment we utter our first cry, and instantly mother puts her breast in our mouth. For the next twenty years we labor under that illusion. All unconscious, granted. Only in the industrialized and technological west could such an illusion persist. In the big scheme of things, none of us is all that important. Recognition of that reality is the beginning of humility."

I stayed silent.

Next he wrote, "You — not in control!" and said, "You are not in control. Most of us learn this the hard way. It is like our sense of importance. We run around thinking we are little gods who control our own destiny. It takes some pretty tough reality checks to shake us out of this illusion. But life is designed to do just that. It might not happen till midlife, but eventually it sinks in. If it hasn't happened before you have children, the onset of their adolescence usually brings a parent back to reality quickly." He smiled as he said this.

"I've been through it once and have another on the way," I said.

"And?"

"We had no ability whatsoever to control our daughter. I'm still operating under the premise that maybe my son will be different."

"Fat chance," was all he said.

Finally, he wrote, "Life — not about you!" "Every young man needs to know that there is a bigger purpose for one's life than one's own gratification. It is not an easy lesson to learn, and in our culture, some never figure this one out.

"I think these concepts should be a part of every young man's initiation — which, unfortunately, most young men will never experience."

We spent the next hour discussing Monroe's model. Monroe believed that at the point of initiation, a boy is taught that one day the ascent will be over, and it will be time to descend. When that time comes, the experiential truth of much of what he learned in initiation begins to guide him through the crisis. Without this preparation, crisis will create immense confusion and misunderstanding.

He also told me that if I really wanted to understand crisis and descent, I needed to make a small detour from my Route 66 travel plans and visit a friend of both his and Leppick's who lived in the boonies of the Ozark Mountains. He assured me that the ride alone would be worth the deviation. He also said that his friend not only knew about these things — he was living them.

⊛

It was late when I got back from Monroe's. The rest of my night at the Coral Court was uneventful: no women; no fights. I looked at *The Way of a Pilgrim* lying on the bed and almost started reading. Since I was pretty bushed, I decided to see if I could figure out what Leppick meant when he said that my doubt about prayer really didn't matter. I decided to try to pray myself to sleep. My last conscious thought was, "Lord Jesus Christ, have mercy on me."

The Ozarks

Journal — September 13: *I'm feeling a bit depressed again this morning. Larry says emotions are only neuropeptides — strings of amino acids floating throughout the body attaching to receptors and stimulating electrical charges on neurons. Easy for him to say ... he's a shrink. I think my depression was caused to a great extent by the work. I remember Buechner's story: "Did you choose to enter the ministry on your own, or did you take someone's bad advice?" Wolf made the same choice. I've heard of him. Why he is in the Ozarks and why I should hunt him down is a mystery to me. Joe said Wolf understands the descent better than anyone he knows. Joe also said Wolf might decide not to tell me a thing.*

I pulled out of the Coral Court at eight the next morning. It was another beautiful September morning. The sky was clear and blue. The forecast for the day had temperatures rising to the mid-seventies — great motorcycle weather.

St. Louis had been disappointing. I had thought I might make more of a connection with the past. Instead, it felt more like I had been totally cut off from the past. And maybe that in itself had made the stop worthwhile.

The old highway now followed Interstate 44 out of St. Louis, heading southwest. A piece down the road I would have to exit Route 66 for a while and head into the Ozarks. Since so much of the old highway had been replaced by Interstate along this stretch, the detour sounded appealing. The next major city I wanted to hit was Joplin. There was a Harley dealer there, and I needed to change the oil in the bike. The Ozark loop would make that a two-day trip.

My own memories of Route 66 date primarily from the early sixties. The road itself dates back to the early 1920s when Cyrus Avery, the father of Route 66, began working on a highway that would connect Chicago to Los Angeles, passing through his home state of Oklahoma. Before Avery's time, each state was responsible for its own highways, and the interstate network was merely a dream in the minds of a few adventurous pioneers. Beginning in 1925, under commission from the secretary of agriculture, Avery and his group began to look at existing state roads that could be networked to form an interstate system.

Route 66 officially came into existence in 1926 with 800 miles of paved road and another 1,600 of graded dirt and gravel. It was another twenty years before the road became what someone called, "the symbolic river of the American West in the auto age of the twentieth century." By then Jack Rittenhouse's book, *A Guide Book to Highway 66*, and Nat King Cole's rendition of Bobby Troup's "Get Your Kicks on Route 66" had made it the most famous highway in America.

A half hour out of St. Louis, I passed Six Flags over Mid-America. It reminded me of my son Teddy. He loved roller coasters. I had hated them until I had a son who had no fear. My daughter Stephanie wouldn't get on one until she was nearly twenty. How bizarre to compare my life now with then. I really hate the thought that I woke up this morning with my son living in Albuquerque and me living nowhere.

I pulled off I-44 at the Gray Summit exit. A "Historic Route 66" sign led me to the old highway again. I hadn't eaten anything yet and was beginning to feel hungry, so I decided to stop in Pacific and get a bite to eat. DJ's cafe was located in an old Quonset hut and looked like another one of those "my kind of places."

After breakfast I stayed on the old road for a while. It was a great morning to be on a bike, and it would have been hard to beat my Road King for the stretch of road I was riding. The engine was performing flawlessly as I gently cruised through town after town. Back when Route 66 was called American's Main Street, this stretch of road was notorious. Many families stopped to visit Meramec and Onondaga Caverns, little realizing that before World War II, this stretch of road was a national red-light district. Bootleg liquor and working girls lured truckers into rest stops all along this stretch. The owners of gas stations even offered free girls with every hundred gallons of gasoline, just another example of the ingenuity of the American entrepreneurial spirit.

Some of the descendants of those days must still occupy these towns. The waves I was getting from some of the female inhabitants of towns like St. Claire, Bourbon, Stanton, and Cuba put me into my discipline of the day: "Lord Jesus Christ, have mercy on me." I got the words right, but I'm not sure Leppick would approve of the way I said it.

Just before leaving Cuba, a cute little high-school girl in her "Cuba Tigers" cheerleading outfit waved and gave me an All-American smile. It reminded me of how much I liked the

Harley. I had ridden more sophisticated and higher performance machines in my earlier motorcycling days, but nothing could compare to a Harley for the kind of trip I was on. Something about Harley-Davidson and Route 66 just went together to create a kind of American synchronicity.

At seven hundred pounds, the Road King was not the biggest or heaviest of Harley's touring line. With my 160 pounds and the gear I had packed in the saddlebags, I represented nearly a half-ton of fun rumbling down the road. In 1996, Harley had extended their sequential port fuel injection to the Road King model. I had picked mine up in the spring of '98 from my friends at Rocky Mountain Harley-Davidson.

I had made a few minor modifications to the bike. The tank bore the 100th Anniversary medallion that all 2003 models bore. I had acquired mine through rather dubious means via a friend who worked in the parts department at Rocky Mountain Harley. The exhaust system was custom, as was the ignition system. A few other modifications and the dyno said I had about 95 rear-wheel horsepower; not much by performance-bike standards, but all the juice I needed for a trip like this.

The production of Harley's first bike dated back to 1903 — which was also the year Sigmund Freud began practicing psychoanalysis. I always viewed this as representing two radically different approaches to mental health, birthed in the same year. Harley had its ups and downs through the years. Their success had ebbed and flowed with the economy. It wasn't until the sixties and seventies that the company got into big trouble.

Having lost the war on the battlefield, the Japanese were already beginning to cream us in the marketplace. The motorcycle industry was one of the arenas where we were taking it in the shorts. Harley could not compete with the cheap bikes pouring in from Japan. A sellout to AMF was nearly disastrous, as the manufacturer of golf carts and bowling shoes began to crank out total junk. Hard-core enthusiasts still speak of the AMF years with disdain.

The turnaround came in the early eighties. The hero who saved Harley was none other than Ronald Reagan. It was during his presidency that the management of the motor company cried out for help. Reagan hated to see an American icon go down the tubes at the hands of the Japanese. He instituted the measures that saved Harley and set the stage for a great American success story.

Trade sanctions were placed on the foreign bikes, making Harley competitive. The employees bought the company back from AMF and committed themselves to making a quality American motorcycle, even if it meant limited production numbers. One of the stars of the turnaround was Willie G. Davidson. To look at Willie G. now, with his long hair, beard, and black leather apparel, it is hard to picture him in those days when he wore black horn-rimmed glasses, sported a flat-top, and always appeared in a coat and tie. Willie G. was an executive with an instinctive feel for what could make Harley great again. He eventually headed up the styling and design department of the company. At a time when many voices were calling for an American response to the beginnings of the crotch-rocket phenomena, Willie G. and the board of the company decided to put all their eggs into the nostalgia basket. The Harley design would stay pure American Iron. The V-twin would remain the engine, and cruisers would be Harley's bread and butter. The company's new commitment was to do what Harley had always done, but to do it better. The result was nearly miraculous.

On March 17, 1987, a group of Harley executives arrived in Washington, D.C., for what was more of a brilliant publicity stunt than a serious effort at public policy. They asked the International Trade Commission to remove the sanctions on foreign motorcycles. Harley was ready to compete head-to-head with the foreign invader! Within a short few years, the demand for their bikes was so great it became nearly impossible for the normal guy on the street to even get a new Harley. Most of the following year's production was committed before one motorcycle rolled off the assembly line. After-market prices soared, and scalpers began to do their damage. The frenzy lasted a few years and then settled down.

During these years, the face of the typical Harley-Davidson rider also changed. No longer did modern versions of Marlon

Brando in *The Wild Ones* have exclusive rights to loud pipes and V-Twins. Instead, you had to be a bit older, more mature, and most of all, have the kind of cash flow it took to buy a motorcycle that in many cases was more expensive than the average car. One of my more hard-core biking buddies coined the expression "Cappuccino Cruisers" to describe this new breed of rider.

The Harley story seemed like a metaphor of my life. I'd had my own ups and downs. I was certainly the self-imposed victim of my own AMF days. The real question in my mind was: Who would be the hero that would bail me out? Would there even be one?

Hopefully, another piece of that puzzle could be found in, of all places, Nantucket, Missouri.

At St. James, I hopped back on the interstate and rode the hundred miles to the Lebanon exit. At Lebanon, I detoured from my Route 66 plan and headed south on Missouri Highway 5 to Grovespring. At Grovespring, I needed to take a country road ten miles south to Nantucket. I was now in the heart of the Ozark territory, and the change of scenery from the Interstate was refreshing. This was serious motorcycling terrain. I began to push the Harley through the long, sweeping curves of road that wound through the rolling, wooded hills. There was not another vehicle in sight. Accelerate through the curve; back off down the straightaway. Don't lean to turn the bike; use the physics of counter-steering to keep in the groove. Add some pure country air filling the lungs, invading the sinuses, and supercharging the brain. If you have never been on a motorcycle on a road like this, I don't think I can explain how good this all feels. Add to this a beautiful, early fall day without a cloud in the sky and temperatures that are about as perfect as they get for riding. If you happen to be a lost soul, it doesn't get much better than this.

Once the senior pastor of the prestigious First Covenant Church of St. Louis, Rev. William Wolf now lived the life of a hermit outside the booming metropolis of Nantucket, Missouri. I had tried to get Joe Monroe to tell me what had happened to Wolf, but he had said only that Wolf should tell his own story.

As I slowed down to roll into Nantucket, I had the thought that this would be an easy town to miss. On my right, I rode past an old Philips 66 filling station. It had only two dilapidated pumps out front, one of them adorned with a handmade sign that said, "PAY INSIDE." Next to the filling station stood a small, yellow-brick post office. One solitary mailbox stood sentinel at the curb. Across the street, a Christian Science reading room occupied a rundown house. Next to it stood the general store. The sign above the door said, "Betty's Emporium." My hunch was that it served as a point of contact with civilization for the folks who lived in the woods around the town. I decided to stop and ask directions to Wolf's house.

I pulled in front of the store and shut down the engine. It took a minute to peel myself off the bike. After taking a good stretch to get the blood circulating in the parts of my body that had nearly quit functioning during the last few hours of riding, I walked into the place.

What can I say? It looked like your average general store in a small and nearly forgotten dot on the map. Several locals were shopping, and two men who appeared to be farmers were shooting the breeze with the lady behind the counter. They all looked pleasant enough.

"Hello there," the nice lady said. I figured she might be Betty. She appeared to be in her late forties or early fifties. Streaks of gray highlighted the dark brown hair she wore in a bob. She was wearing a checked, button-down shirt and faded jeans. There on the shirt was the evidence — a small badge that said, "Betty."

"Hi," I said.

The two men didn't say anything. They simply checked me out — thoroughly.

"How can I help you?" Betty asked.

"I'm looking for the house of a fellow named William Wolf," I said.

The two men burst out laughing. I didn't know if this was good or bad. Betty grinned instantly and then forced a disapproving glance to chastise the guys. It was one of those looks where one side of her face was about to laugh while the other was trying to make the laughing side behave itself. It wasn't working.

"Is something the matter?" I asked.

"Not at all," she said. "These boys just don't know how to behave themselves."

"Did I say something funny?" I asked.

"Oh . . . everyone around here just gets a kick out of someone asking about William. He's kind of local celebrity, you might say."

This seemed to make the guys laugh even harder, but eventually they regained their composure.

"And why is that?" I asked.

"You better let William explain it to you. It wouldn't be fair of us to tell his story," she said.

"How do I find him?" I asked.

"That depends on if he's running through the woods naked," the more portly of the two men said. As soon as he said it, all three burst out laughing. I wasn't quite sure how to respond.

"Now stop that, Gene," Betty said. Her performance as custodian of proper social discourse in Nantucket lost a bit of credibility due to the fact that she was giggling when she said it. "He lives just outside town," she said. "Take the left fork off the road that runs from the county highway that heads north off Main Street a few hundred yards after the city park."

By the time I hit the fork, I was in total isolation in the woods. The fork put me on a little dirt road that ended at a small log cabin. If Betty's directions and my navigation skills were both functioning properly, this was where Wolf lived. If you like isolation, there was no question that you would have loved the Reverend's retirement haven.

I was a bit hesitant to make this stop. Monroe had not told me much about what Wolf was doing these days, but I remembered him by reputation from my own days as a man of the cloth. He was legendary in certain theological circles. A fellow classmate of the late Francis Schaeffer at Covenant Theological Seminary in St. Louis, Wolf took the senior position at First Covenant after a number of successful pastorates in small churches around the Midwest. At First Covenant, he had become one of the shining stars of the St. Louis ecclesiastical community. I hadn't known, until Joe told me, that he had retired, but then I had been pretty much out of touch with the church world for the last few years.

My fear was that Wolf would try to lay a trip on me about obedience and calling and family and every other thing that was potentially a source of guilt in my life. I had heard it all before. It hadn't helped. But I had promised Monroe I would come, and he had promised me that, if nothing else, I would love the ride through the Ozarks. On that point, he was absolutely accurate.

I had barely shut down the Harley when a tall, distinguished-looking gentleman appeared. I experienced immediate cognitive dissonance, related somehow to the stark contrast between the dignified face and bearing of the man on the porch and the faded overalls and worn-out T-shirt he wore underneath. This didn't quite look like the William Wolf of legendary reputation.

"Hello," Wolf said quietly from his place on the porch. "I assume you are the friend Joe called about. If not, it is quite a coincidence to have two Harley riders find my hideout in the same day."

"I'm the one," I said as I climbed off the bike and stretched. "You really live out in the boonies!"

"That's the whole point, my friend."

"Why Nantucket?" I asked as I walked up the steps of the cabin to the porch where Wolf stood.

"Actually, my car broke down on my way to nowhere, and while I waited for a part to be shipped, I fell in love with the serenity of the place," he said as he extended his hand. "William Wolf, but just call me Bill."

"John Calvin. So where is 'nowhere'?" I asked as I shook it.

"Joe didn't tell you my story, I take it?"

"No. Actually, he acted a bit strange when I asked about you. He said it would be better for you to tell me yourself."

"Sounds like Joe. He was the only friend I had in the world at one time. I probably would not have agreed to meet with you if it had been anyone other than Joe Monroe who asked. Since he knows how I feel about things, I will assume that you must be a pretty special fellow for him to even ask."

"I don't think so. Just a lost soul looking for a few answers," I said, a bit too nonchalantly.

"I'm not sure I can help with that, but come on in and have a bite to eat. I made us lunch."

The cabin was made of log and stone. Its interior was stark. The large living area contained a kitchen and a living room with a stone fireplace. The furnishings were spartan.

A handmade wooden table with four simple chairs sat opposite the kitchen, transforming raw space into a dining area. Facing the fireplace were two well-worn, overstuffed chairs. Unlike the Monroe and Leppick homes, Wolf's living room contained no bookshelves loaded with scholarly volumes. An obviously well-used Bible sat on a round table next to one of the chairs. It was the only book in sight.

"If you'd like to wash your hands before lunch, you'll find a bath down the hall," he said, pointing toward the rear of the cabin.

While washing, I looked in the mirror at the face that belonged to me. The hair was too long for the current style. The beard that covered the lower part of my face was relatively well trimmed. Both were getting faint traces of gray. I am told I have one of those deceptive faces that makes me appear younger than I actually am. In early adulthood, I was always trying to convince people that I was older than they thought. Now I was beginning to enjoy being mistaken for someone in his thirties. My friends who had become victims of the dreaded male-pattern baldness liked to enviously harass me about my "bionic" hair, still thick and with no sign of receding. Good hair genes were the only positive quality I seemed to have inherited. My ball cap had crushed my hair into respectable position, so I splashed some cold water onto my face, dried my hands, and headed back to the kitchen.

I found the table set and Wolf coming from the kitchen with a steaming pot hanging from one hand and a soup ladle in the other. The table contained a loaf of bread, a chunk of cheese, and a bottle of what looked like homemade wine.

"I hope you will find this adequate," Wolf said. "I eat quite simply these days."

"It looks great," I replied. "The bread looks homemade. Did you make it?"

"No. I get it from a neighbor. He used to own a bakery in New York City. Moved here after being shot in the chest during his fifth armed robbery. The bullet lodged an inch from the heart."

"How about the wine? Local bootleggers?" I asked facetiously.

"Another neighbor. He was a banker in Kansas City. Now he has a small vineyard down the road."

"Sounds like you have some pretty interesting folks living around here."

"You'd be amazed. These hills hold many stories."

"Sounds like you have one yourself," I said.

"Not a very pretty one, I'm afraid."

"Does it have something to do with being on the way to nowhere?" I asked.

"I haven't decided if I'm going to tell you," he said. He gently let the ladle plunge into the pot and withdrew a full measure of the soup. He poured it into my bowl.

I waited for him to fill his own bowl and be seated before I spoke again.

"Joe warned me that you might not spill the beans," I said, digging into the soup and cheese. "This is great, by the way."

"Thank you," he said. He hesitated for a few seconds and then looked me in the eye. He smiled.

I stopped eating. He began his story.

❀

"I think you already know I was the senior pastor at First Covenant. It was the pinnacle of ecclesiastical success in our denomination, and I held the position with a bit of professional pride, although in public I'm sure I always presented a picture of appropriate humility. I had a number of books published and was on the adjunct faculty at Covenant Seminary. We had a lovely home in Clayton and were the picture of the ideal family."

"Sounds familiar," I said.

"Yes, I understand that we were on quite similar tracks," Wolf replied.

"I destroyed mine," I said, without flinching from his stare.

"So did I," Wolf answered.

"You're kidding," I said stupidly.

"Not at all," he said, then continued. "I was living a lie. My life was so filled with activity and falseness, I think I even had myself fooled. As you know, I'm sure, the occupational hazard of the clergy is to articulate spiritual realities with which you yourself have lost touch."

I knew exactly what he meant.

"The greater my so-called success, the lonelier and more isolated I became. My marriage was in horrible shape. Fortunately, by the time I reached the height of my career, the children were grown and away at school.

"First Covenant ran like a Fortune 500 company. It was a well-oiled machine. My executive assistant made sure that I was insulated from the normal day-to-day operation of the church. Slowly but surely, I distanced myself from anyone who could have detected what was going on in my life or hold me personally accountable for the state of my spiritual and emotional health."

"What about your wife?" I asked.

"She knew. Unfortunately, I had managed to slowly distance myself from her, also. I was present physically but always a million miles away emotionally. The relationship became very dissatisfying to both of us.

"At some point, I began to lose control. I had no authentic inner life. I depended on old material for sermons. It was a charade, but I couldn't let go. Internally, the frustration was building at the same time that the energy was running out. I began to want out desperately. That's when Miss Crane came along."

I knew what was coming before he said a word. "Hey, you don't have to go into all this," I said.

"Don't you want to hear the gory details?"

"Not if you don't want to tell me."

"I don't," he said. "But I probably should. It is humiliating. And sometimes humiliation is good for the soul."

I had the sense that it was with no small measure of reluctance that he continued.

"Alice Crane was a young seminary graduate we hired to run our early childhood learning center. I was the final link in the hiring process, and our interview went quite well. I felt a certain connection with her from the beginning. In retrospect, I'm sure it was nothing more than physical attraction.

"Although I had virtually no contact with the other staff, I began to take a special interest in Alice, as she obviously did with me. Periodically, she would drop by my office to ask for advice on some issue. I always seemed to have time to see her. She was extremely competent and quite attractive. I should have stopped spending time with her when I became aware of the attraction I felt and recognized it for what it was, but to be honest, I didn't have the will or the energy to resist. I desperately wanted what I was feeling when I was with her.

"I'm sure you know where this is going, so I'll cut to the chase. I had been invited to be a keynote speaker at the annual convention of the National Association of Evangelicals. Margaret, my wife, didn't care to come. I traveled alone, a dangerous practice, particularly for a man in my state of emotional disrepair.

"Alice was also attending the convention. It was held at the downtown Hilton in San Francisco. Most of the people attending the conference stayed there. I justified my choice of a smaller and more intimate hotel around the corner by my need for privacy to prepare for my address. But in my heart, I knew that I was preparing for something quite different.

"Alice sat on the front row at the meeting, looking up at me with admiring and affirming body language. Afterward we went out for coffee. I walked her back to the hotel and took a cab to mine. Within fifteen minutes, there was a knock at the door of my room. It was Alice. She asked if she could come in, and I made the mistake of saying yes. She was trembling, and the look on her face had such focused intensity. I asked her what was wrong, and with great honesty, she told me she was sure I knew what was wrong."

Tears began to form in Wolf's eyes.

"You don't need to go on," I said.

"No. I *do* need to go on," he said. "She drew near and fixed her gaze on me. I reached out, knowing it was so wrong. I wanted to stop, and I didn't want to stop. As usual in these situations, desire trumped character. I took her in my arms, drew her to myself, and kissed her. I picked her up off the ground and carried her to the bed. I had not felt passion like this in years. I was like a wild beast."

He began to weep. "There was one last moment of decision. I knew this was horribly wrong, but I wanted it so badly. In a split second I made the choice. We committed adultery."

Wolf quit crying and settled down. He remained silent for a moment and then continued. "When it was over, we both lay silently, holding each other. I don't think either of us knew what to say. She began telling me how much she loved me. I told her the same, although even then it sounded hollow. I knew it wasn't about love.

"I awoke about six in the morning and knew that my life, as I knew it, was over. When Alice finally drifted into consciousness, she looked like a frightened child. Like a total fool, I told her I was going to divorce my wife and marry her. She threw her arms around me and again told me how much she loved me and needed me."

Wolf stopped speaking. Telling the story had obviously been emotionally draining.

"Then what?" I asked.

"I endured the longest plane flight of my life back to St. Louis," he quietly reflected. "I went immediately home and told my wife exactly what had happened. I called the head of the church board and told him I was submitting my resignation, effective immediately, and that I would explain why later. Then I went to the basement of my house and loaded a shotgun. I put the barrel into my mouth and reached for the trigger."

Wolf paused. After several moments he continued, "I couldn't do it."

Wolf looked up and beyond me.

"Would you excuse me for a few minutes?" he asked. Then he walked out the door and into the woods.

I sat stunned for several minutes, then realized I had not touched my lunch since he began speaking.

"Dang!" I said, pouring another glass of wine.

❀

Nearly an hour later, Wolf returned to the cabin. There was a marked change in his countenance. It was as if somehow, on his walk, he had come to terms once again with the story he had just told. I had spent the time enjoying the lunch he had prepared and then sitting on the cabin's porch, listening to the quiet.

He climbed the stairs with a smile and said, "Sorry about that. Remembering the whole affair is still a bit overwhelming."

"You don't have to say more," I said. Then I added, "But you did leave yourself in the basement with a shotgun in your mouth."

We walked back inside and settled into the two chairs by the fireplace. Wolf turned his a bit so that we were facing each other.

"I would be lying if I told you I wasn't curious about what happened next," I said.

"Grace happened," Wolf said. "I couldn't pull the trigger. I didn't have the courage, or someone I couldn't see stopped me. I put the gun down and walked upstairs and out of the house. I got in my car and started driving. I made it as far as Nantucket when my car broke down."

"The trip to nowhere," I said.

"Exactly. After making arrangements to get the car fixed, I walked into the woods. I got lost. I stayed out here for three days. Charles Williams once wrote a book titled *Descent into Hell*."

"I've read it," I said.

"It would be a fitting title for what I went through those three days in the woods."

BOB BELTZ

"What happened?" I asked.

"Before I tell you, let me ask what you know of the male spiritual journey," he said. "Joe said you and he had talked at length about it."

"I have this piece of paper I've been taking notes on," I said as I pulled out my diagram from Monroe. "Dr. Monroe added some to what Professor Leppick explained to me."

Wolf smiled at the worn piece of paper. "Julius," he said with a smile. "A great man — and a good friend. He and Joe like to try to make these things fit into neat little categories and diagrams. The whole process is not so black and white." He paused, then said, "Perhaps you might like a fresh piece of paper to add another element to your schematic."

He reached for the Bible sitting on the table and pulled out a pad of paper. He turned to a blank page and prepared to write.

"Tell me what you understand so far," he said.

I told him what Leppick had told me about the ascent, descent, and crisis, and Monroe about initiation. He rapidly sketched the diagram from my old scrap of paper. It looked neater in Wolf's handwriting.

"There is another piece that is not on your sketch," he said. Right at the top of the ascent, and before the crisis, there is a point that is critical. He drew in a new circle and labeled it "Identity."

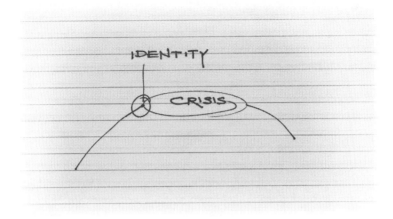

"Without understanding the period of self-identity, it is very hard to understand why we go into crisis and what the descent is all about," he explained. "The period of identity usually begins sometime in our thirties. It is the culmination of the years of ascent, from the time when initiation should have occurred until we reach this point," he said, pointing to the circle.

"At the point of self-identity, theoretically, we have developed a relatively stable sense of who we are. We have been defined, and we have usually come to some resolution about our definition of self."

Wolf paused to see if I was getting what he was saying. I tried to act like I got it.

"The problem with this sense of self is that it is false," he continued. "It gives us an identity that is the product of what we have either accomplished or failed to accomplish during the ascent. For most men in our culture, it is the product of what we have accumulated in material possessions, the size of our income, what vocational position we hold, and how others view our success.

"In my own case, it was all that went along with being the senior pastor of First Covenant Church. Everyone in my little fishbowl told me I had arrived. My hunch is that *your* identity was derived from similar input."

"Probably," I said.

"This period can last a long time. For some men, it involves ten or twenty years of living with a false sense of who they are. The more successful a man is in terms of what culture defines as success, the more likely he is to lock into this false self and stay stuck in it. That is, unless God is at work in his life."

"What do you mean?" I asked.

"Let me take you back to the woods. It might help you understand," he replied.

"I think you were about to descend into hell."

"Sometimes, hell is exactly what we need. Even the psalmist said, 'If I descend into Sheol, even there you are with me.'"

"I feel like I just spent five years there," I said.

"That's just the point. We spend years on the fringes, not letting ourselves really plunge into the depths. I had been living in what I thought was hell, only to discover it was really more like Lewis's Gray City. I was creating a personal hell that pushed me over the edge into the real thing. But in my case, the real thing was the only hope I had of being saved."

"You just lost me," I said.

"My whole life had become false. I was a big fake trying to play the role of the Holy Man. I was living a lie and had turned it into my existential truth. Look where it got me.

"In the woods I was confronted with my self. I believe I had — well, actually, I should say I know I had — an encounter with God. Twenty-six years in professional ministry without one real experience, and God meets me in the woods of Missouri when I have just totally flushed my life down the toilet."

"I'm still not sure I really get what you are saying," I said.

"This is the part that is really hard to explain. By the end of the second day in the woods, I found myself in a state of emotional agony beyond description. I saw it all. Who I really was, what I had done, why I had done it, and how absolutely repulsive and hideous it was. At first it was just all in my head, but then night came. I became frightened. All the barriers were coming down. I rolled up in fetal position and started crying. I was in very bad shape."

"Yeah. . . . " I started to say something stupid, then stopped myself.

Wolf went on. "This is what the crisis is all about. The floor falls out from under you. You realize that nothing that used to work, works. You feel your life crumbling beneath you. That is, if you are lucky."

There was conviction in Wolf's voice as he described the experience. He might have been nuts, but one thing was certain, the experience had been real to him, and it still moved him to tell of it.

"I cried myself to sleep that night. When I woke, it started all over again. An observer would probably have thought I was having an emotional breakdown, but what I was having was deeper. If you believe in a baptism of fire, I was having it. John of the Cross called it Purgation. Others have called it the Great Defeat.

"I reached a point sometime that morning where I began to cry out to God to take my life. I already knew I didn't have what it took to kill myself. But I wanted to die.

"That's when the experience took a new direction. I realized that, if I was being totally honest, I didn't want to die. I was still being false before God. So I began to tell God what I *really* wanted. I don't remember the exact details, but it was something about wanting to rule the world and have sex with the entire Dallas Cowboys cheerleading squad."

"Now that sounds like a religious experience," I blurted, like a stupid adolescent.

"It actually was," Wolf replied with complete sincerity. "For the first time in years, I was being honest with myself and God. God had cut through the illusion.

"What I had really been longing for all my life, playing the good boy and the religious game, I found lying in a heap in the woods of the Ozarks."

"Which was?"

"Grace. I found grace."

"I still don't get it," I said.

"That was the next encounter. After the fire came the grace. Sometime during the morning of my—what shall I call it—confession, I began to experience a very gentle sense of a presence. The presence seemed to penetrate all the filters of my consciousness and engage me at the core of my being. When this happened, I felt love. Pure love. I believe it was God."

"I'm not—" I began.

"Shh." Wolf put his finger to his lips. "I told you the worst, now let me tell you what saved my life. God made himself known to me in the most interior part of my being, and what I experienced was love. This is grace. It doesn't get any clearer than that. Be a phony, commit adultery, attempt suicide, run away, get lost in the woods, tell God you want the cheerleaders, and get love. That, my friend, is grace."

"No kidding," I said, not sure how to respond.

"No kidding at all."

"So what happened after that?" I asked.

"It was getting late in the day by then. I fell back into a deep sleep. When I awoke it was dark. I was lost in the woods and hungry, and I felt more alive and real than I ever had in my life. I had this strange sense that everything was going to be all right.

"I started wandering in the woods in the dark. I heard every sound of the woods and felt the breeze against my face. I decided to take off my clothes. I felt like I was in perfect harmony with the universe." Wolf stopped when he saw my face. "I told you this was hard to describe. It sounds like some raving lunatic running through the woods, doesn't it?"

"Actually, it does sound pretty strange."

"Sanity returns in a moment," he assured me. "Hang with me here. I slept naked in the woods."

"Let me guess—and you woke up without even a chigger bite," I suggested.

"Nope," Wolf said with a huge grin. "I got eaten alive by chiggers and ticks and bit by a rattlesnake."

"You're kidding!"

"Not a bit. I was near death when the search party found me. I had only wandered about a mile from town. They rushed me to the hospital in Joplin."

"So did you have one of those Billy Jack, rattlesnake-type of visions?" I asked.

"No. I was as sick as I had ever been in my life. I laid in a hospital bed in Joplin for two weeks without another hint of a spiritual experience."

"Then what happened?"

"They called my wife."

"And?"

"She said she wished I had died and to send me back to the woods to try again," he answered.

"What did you do?"

"I knew she was mad as hell, and she had the right to be. So I decided not to push my luck. They also called my children, who said about the same thing as my wife. I figured my old life was over and that I would just take it one day at a time. I began the descent," he said as he pointed to the downward line on the diagram. "I was lucky. It takes some men years in crisis before they get it. Some never do. I guess you could say I got it in one big night in the woods!"

"So how did you end up back here?" I asked.

"I came back to Nantucket to get my car. The part had still not arrived. It was pretty clear that everyone knew about my little adventure. I couldn't walk down the street without giggles and sneers from everyone in town.

"The waitress at the cafe was the only person who seemed to feel sorry for me. I told her a very condensed version of my story, and she suggested I rent a room for a few nights. That was three years ago."

"That's a long time to wait for a part!" I joked.

"The part came. But by the end of the week, I had rented this cabin and sold the car. I went into the woods every day and walked and thought. I decided I needed a much undeserved sabbatical to put my life back together."

"And have you?" I asked.

"I'm working on it," Wolf replied with a smile. "I'm still in process. I'm descending."

"What about your wife and kids?" I asked.

"She divorced me."

"And the kids?"

"The kids were already out of the house before this happened. They've both been down to see me. We have made our peace."

"I wish I could say the same."

"Has your wife divorced you?" he asked.

"Actually, I divorced her."

"Oh, I see," he said with a puzzled look. "Are there any children?"

"My daughter is married. She told me she never wants to speak to me again. My son is eleven. I try to stay in touch with him. He still doesn't understand the whole thing."

"That's a pretty tough age to not have a dad," Wolf observed.

I didn't respond.

"Would you like a drink?" he asked.

"Sure, how about a little more of that Ozark moonshine?"

"I like to think of it as Nantucket Cabernet."

I spent an hour walking in the woods. I tried to process what Wolf had told me about his experience in the woods, but it was hard. It might have all been psychological. It might have been authentic. I had no way to evaluate. All the talk about descent and how falling apart is a good thing still didn't connect with where I was.

When I returned to the cabin, William had fixed a dinner of roasted chicken and fresh vegetables.

We ate in silence. I didn't know whether Wolf wanted me to spill the beans on my disaster, but I wasn't really up to it. I guess he sensed as much, because he didn't push.

"Where are you headed from here?" Wolf asked.

"On down Route 66," I replied.

"All the way to California?"

"I don't know. I'm taking it one day at a time."

"That can be a great way to live," he offered tentatively.

"I'm waiting for the 'but,'" I said.

"Or it can be hellish," he said.

"What makes the difference?"

"I guess that's what you are looking for," Wolf replied.

Kansas

Journal — September 14: I leave Missouri today and head across the tip of Kansas, then on into Oklahoma. The time with Wolf was both challenging and troubling. He told me he agreed with Leppick and Monroe about my state of crisis. No kidding! The big question is whether I will ever get out of it. I'm not really sure I like the idea of descent. I'm actually still not quite sure I understand what it means. Where does it lead? What happens on the way down? What if I just decide not to go there? Where do Elizabeth and the kids fit into all this? I have more questions today than I did when I left Chicago!

I had mixed feelings pulling out of Nantucket the next morning. I would have liked to have had an encounter like Wolf's — one that might have kept me there for years. The problem, of course, is that those kinds of experiences can't be orchestrated. As William said, it was grace. If God has a hand, it can't be forced. Since I had experienced no divine intervention, it was back to the road.

Not wanting to get back on the Interstate just yet, I dropped down Highway 5 until it intersected US 60 and headed west into Springfield. Since I wanted to get the bike's oil changed in Joplin, I hopped back on I-44 and made the seventy-mile trip in under an hour.

While they changed the oil at the Harley shop, I walked across the street and grabbed a burger at an old Tastee Freeze. After wolfing down my burger and polishing off a large vanilla milkshake, I spread-eagled myself on top of a picnic table under the shade of a huge oak and drifted to sleep to the sound of the breeze gently rustling through the leaves. The next thing I knew, the mechanic from the shop was shaking me awake to let me know the bike was ready.

As soon as I regained a reasonable amount of consciousness, I bid Joplin adieu and headed west. I hadn't been back on the road much more than ten minutes when I crossed the Missouri state line and began rolling down the 13.2 miles of old Route 66 that cuts across the southeastern tip of Kansas.

Kansas evoked a few memories. Although I hadn't lived anywhere near Route 66, I had lived in Kansas as a child. My family moved here after St. Louis and a year in Ponca City, Oklahoma.

I'd lived in Russell, Kansas — Bob Dole country. 1523 Elm St. I don't remember a great deal about those years, except my parents not getting along. I was ten when they split up. Family systems people would probably point to those years as providing the foundation for my own marital disaster.

I'm grateful that Route 66 cuts through only a corner of the state, because six hundred miles of flat, straight roads is not my idea of fun.

I had just passed through Galena when I saw her. I spoke my variation of the Jesus Prayer: "Lord, have mercy." I'm not in the habit of picking up hitchhikers, but any red-blooded American male would have at least entertained the idea of stopping for this one. Seeing this particular woman hitchhiking immediately created such a sense of curiosity that I had to stop just to find out what in the world she was up to. I downshifted, put on my signal, and headed for the shoulder of the road.

She was cute. I had her pegged in her late twenties or early thirties. She was dressed in faded jeans and a brown leather jacket. As I got closer, I could see that her cowboy boots matched the jacket, and both were obviously expensive. Under her jacket, she wore a simple bright red T-shirt. Did a woman who dressed like that really need to be standing on the outskirts of some remote Kansas town with her thumb out?

"Hi," I said, as she moved toward the bike, "I'm John."

"Hi John, I'm Nikki," she said.

She had a nice smile. All I could think to say was, "Are you really hitchhiking?"

She laughed and shook her head as if she didn't believe it herself. "Yes, I'm really hitchhiking."

"Why?" As soon as I said it, I realized it was none of my business and probably sounded pretty stupid.

"It's a long story," she said.

"I'd like to hear it."

"I bet you would." I could tell she had a nice sense of humor.

"So, where are you heading?" I asked.

"West. How about you?"

"West," I replied. I hesitated for a moment, remembering that I intended to avoid female distraction on this pilgrimage, but with the same resolve and self-control that had marked the last few years of my life, I asked, "Want a lift?"

She thought about it, checking out the bike and the biker. With a slight hesitation, she replied, "I'm not sure. I was thinking car, not motorcycle." Then she asked, "Are you safe?"

Good question, I thought. What I said was, "Safe? I'm not sure, but I'm good."

She thought for a moment, then said, "Interesting answer."

"*The Lion, the Witch and the Wardrobe,*" I said.

"Lucy to Mr. Beaver," she said in reply, as she handed me her bag — obviously intending to take me up on my offer.

"Are you a Lewis fan?" I asked as I got off the Harley and took her leather duffel. It strapped easily on top of the one I had secured to my luggage rack. Wherever she planned on going, she was traveling light.

"I'm a teacher," she answered. "Fifth grade. Every fifth grader should know about Aslan. Don't you think?"

"Absolutely." I got back on the bike, and she climbed on behind me. "Do you hitchhike a lot?"

"Never," she said.

I fired up the bike and headed down the road.

❁

If you've never engaged in conversation on a motorcycle, you probably don't know how intimate it can be when you're not constrained by a helmet. Nikki's body was pressed close to mine as we talked. She had her arms wrapped around my torso, and her chin was just above my right shoulder. In this position her mouth was only inches from my ear. Within minutes we were engaged in spirited conversation. We crossed into Oklahoma before I thought to wish Kansas farewell.

"By the way," I said as we crossed the state line, "If you're not eighteen, I may have just committed a federal crime."

"Don't worry," she replied. "You're safe by over a decade."

"I take it you're not from that little town back there?" I asked.

"Nope," she answered. "Chicago."

"What in the world were you doing in Galena, Kansas?"

"I've been traveling old Route 66 and decided to hitch for a day or two, hoping to meet someone interesting to travel with. I have to admit I was thinking car, maybe old 'Vette like on the TV show."

"I think you're a bit young to remember that show."

"Let's just say I had a friend who turned me on to the best of archaic Americana."

"Careful," I responded. "You're traveling with a bit of that archaic Americana, and I may be sensitive."

"In my limited experience, the overly sensitive types don't ride Harleys and definitely don't pick up female hitchhikers."

I liked her.

Northeastern Oklahoma delightfully defied my Oklahoma stereotype. Oklahoma had always conjured in my mind flat, desolate dust bowls, à la Steinbeck's *The Grapes of Wrath*. This part of the state was a pleasant extension of the Ozark country of Southwestern Missouri. The old road wound its way up and over rolling hills covered with lush foliage. The road conformed to the topography in a way modern highways seldom do. The rolling landscape was interrupted every ten miles or so by another little jewel of a town.

I slowed the bike as we hit the outskirts of Commerce.

"I think we should observe a moment of silence," I said.

"Why's that?"

I pointed to a billboard by the side of the road that proclaimed, "Commerce. Boyhood home of Mickey Mantle."

"He was great, I hear," she said. "Not quite as great as Sammy Sosa."

"Spoken like a true Chicagoan," I said.

Three miles down the road we came to Miami. The road ran through the center of a town that looked as if it had been preserved in a time freeze dating back to the fifties. After Miami, we passed rapidly through Narcissa, Afton, Vinita, White Oak, and Chelsea on what the locals call the Free Road. We were now deep in the heart of Will Rogers country. Nikki was filled with little details about the stretch we were on. In every small town, people smiled and waved. This is the heart of middle America, and one can only be grateful that Will grew up here, "between Claremore and Oolagah" as he used to say. Had it been somewhere like midtown Manhattan, we might be stuck with the idiom "I never met a man I actually liked," rather than the more positive cliché old Will left us.

About 10:45, I asked, "Would you like to stop in Tulsa and get a cup of coffee?"

"I never drink the stuff," she replied. "But let's get through Tulsa quick and stop in Sapulpa."

"Sa what sa?" I asked.

"Sapulpa. Trust me," she said.

"Sapulpa it is," I said, twisting the throttle on the Road King.

Just east of Tulsa, we hopped on I-44 and took it to the Turner Turnpike heading south. Sure enough, fourteen miles down the road we came to an exit for Sapulpa, Oklahoma.

"Anywhere in particular you'd like to go in Sapulpa?" I asked with a hint of sarcasm.

"Follow the signs to Route 66 and look for Norma's Cafe," she instructed.

"How in the world —" I began, but she interrupted.

"I read about it in a book."

The sign in the window of Norma's Cafe was a classic: "WOW! BREAKFAST 99 cents." We sat at a table by the window, and before I had a chance to ask a question, Norma herself had descended upon us.

"What'll it be today?" she asked in an efficient, yet friendly, voice.

"I was just going to have coffee, but I'm not sure I can pass up a ninety-nine cent breakfast," I said.

"If you're really hungry, you better have the Tower of Power," she suggested.

"And what, pray tell, is the Tower of Power?" I asked.

With a big grin Norma fired off, "Scrambled eggs, bacon, cheese, and the works, all piled high on a piece of Texas toast."

"The old heart-attack special," I joked.

"Well, folks around here been eatin' it for nearly forty years and still live to be older than dirt," Norma responded, defending her obviously beloved cuisine.

"Actually, I already had breakfast, but my friend here might take you up on that . . . "

"Tower of Power," Norma completed my sentence. "How about it, honey?" she asked. "Could we put a little meat on them bones?"

"No thank you, but I could use a cup of tea, if you have any, and what do you have that's sweet?" Nikki asked.

"We've got Celestial Seasonings if you want herbal, or Earl Grey if you prefer regular, and the homemade chocolate pie is to die for," Norma explained. "It's my granddaughter's favorite."

"It sounds wonderful," Nikki said. "I'll have the Earl Grey and a piece of the pie."

"How about you, Captain?" Norma asked as she wrote Nikki's order on her pad.

"My Grandma used to call me that," I said.

"Smart lady, obviously," Norma said.

"She was my favorite person on the planet when I was a child," I explained.

"That's what grandmas are for, honey," Norma replied. "Now, how 'bout I bring you something, and you pretend I'm that grandma of yours?" Norma suggested.

"Coffee, with cream and sugar, and a piece of the famous chocolate pie, Grams," I ordered.

"Coming right up, Captain."

As soon as Norma left, I turned my attention to the lady sitting across the table. I was surprised to see that she was not only looking at me, but doing so in a way that suggested careful scrutiny. Probably trying to figure out what kind of guy I was. In contrast, I was checking out the configuration of Nikki's various body parts. I actually tried to keep my eyes on her eyes, but I know they drifted. I honestly think most men can't help it. She was really cute — not beautiful, but cute. I tried to focus.

"So tell me about Nikki-who-never-hitchhikes-except-for-today-in-the-most-obscure-regions-of-Kansas," I asked.

"Can you be trusted?" she asked.

Fortunately, she was smiling when she asked the question.

It was a bit like the previous "safe" question, but this time nothing from Narnia came to my mind. "I don't know," I answered.

"The last honest man in America!"

"Not really," I said.

"Humility, too," she chided.

"Give me a break!"

"I was just kidding," she said. "I'm not quite sure where to begin. Okay, I'm twenty-nine, divorced, and working on my PhD in Sociology at the University of Chicago while I teach fifth grade."

"I'm impressed," I said. "You are also lovely, mysterious, and a bit nuts to be hitchhiking in the dawn of the new millennium here in America."

"Like I said, I have never hitched a ride in my life until today."

"So how did you end up outside Galena, Kansas?"

"I'm doing my dissertation on the culture of old Route 66. I hopped on a bus in Chicago and decided to go as far as time and budget allow."

"Ergo, Sapulpa, Oklahoma and Norma's Cafe?" I asked rhetorically.

"You've got it."

Norma appeared with tea, coffee, and two pieces of the most outrageous looking chocolate pie I had seen in years.

"Here you go, kids. *Bon appétit!*" Norma said. The expression had a whole new vibe when spoken with an Oklahoma accent.

"Watch out," I cautioned Nikki. "This will not enhance that petite figure of yours."

"I've noticed you seem to have thoroughly scrutinized it," she said with a grin.

This is another fact about the mating habits of the species. We might think they don't know we are checking them out, but they do. Most just never acknowledge it.

"I apologize," I said.

"I'm just kidding," she said. "I'm used to it. It's the dilemma of having the genetic makeup that happens to coincide with whatever the prevailing cultural definition of beauty happens to be. Thirty years ago, I would have been considered too skinny," she stated with academic authority, while digging into the mass of pie in front of her.

"Trust me," I responded. "Thirty years ago you still would have stopped traffic!"

"And you're real cute for an old guy on a motorcycle."

"Thanks a lot!" I said.

"Oh, you are the sensitive type," she mocked, emphasizing the "are."

"Enough! Back to the saga," I said.

"I grew up in Chicago," she began. "Dad was a high school teacher, and Mom was the most wonderful woman in the world. They're both gone. I miss them terribly.

"We had a nice life, and I was a happy girl. Then I made a few mistakes." I could sense the shift in tone in her voice.

"What happened?" I asked.

"I got pregnant my senior year. It's a long story, and you really don't want to hear it. Trust me."

I actually would have liked to hear it, but I acted like she was right.

"My boyfriend and I," she continued, "had dated through most of high school. When we found out I was pregnant, he wanted to get married. His parents nearly demanded it. Mine were heartbroken, but supportive. They told me that I needed to make the decision."

"What about an abortion?" I asked.

"I was pro-life."

"At seventeen?" I asked.

"I had strong convictions."

"Except with your boyfriend," I said. I was sorry I'd said it the minute it stupidly tumbled out of my mouth.

"Careful!"

"Sorry."

"I'm probably overly sensitive because it ruined my life for years — three to be exact."

"Not happily-ever-after, I take it."

"It was a nightmare. He was a total jerk from day one. I didn't understand the concept of emotional and verbal abuse, but the night he knocked my front tooth out, I decided I'd better do something. It was about this time that I discovered I had chlamydia. Since I hadn't had sex with anyone but Mr. Wonderful, my suspicions were confirmed that on top of everything else he was fooling around."

"I hope you don't mind me saying that this guy must have been an absolute fool."

"Someone once said that most of the problems in America are caused by stupid, young males," she observed.

"Could be," I said. "So what did you do?"

"Divorced him and moved back home. I went to junior college and worked my tail off as a waitress. At the end of two years I was awarded a scholarship to the University of Chicago. I graduated cum laude and was given a graduate assistant position in the Department of Sociology while I worked on my master's. After that I started teaching fifth grade and began work on my PhD. That pretty much summarizes the last seven years of my life."

"Which brings us to Galena, Kansas, and one dissertation on Route 66?" I asked.

"Actually, it's about the sociological phenomena created by the sense of nostalgia surrounding this old road. I assume you are riding it for some kind of nostalgic flashback to a better time in your life?" she asked.

"Your first missed assumption," I said. "At least I now know you are fallible. By the way, have you ever had chocolate pie any better than this?"

"Yep. My mom's."

"Can I come home with you?"

"That might be a bit premature, but as I said before, Mom and Dad are gone."

"I'm sorry, I forgot."

"Good. Then we are both fallible. But I might take you home anyway, if you're lucky," she teased.

"How are you kids doin'?" it was Norma, back with more coffee and hot water.

"Norma, you are a culinary genius!" I said. "I have never in all my pie-eating life tasted anything like this."

"Then why didn't you finish it?" Norma asked, pretending to be incensed.

"I'm stuffed."

"Didn't your momma ever tell you to clean your plate?"

"Oh, yeah. She was always telling me stuff like that. Mind if I ask you a question?"

"Fire away."

"I've been riding old Route 66 for a few days now, and most of the old places are shut down. How have you managed to stay in business?"

"Too stubborn to quit."

"Do you get enough business to make it?"

"The turnpike and the fast-food places really hurt us. We've got all of 'em — McDonald's, Burger King, Arby's, Wendy's — anything you want except good food. Used to be we'd be open 6 a.m. till midnight, six days a week. Anymore, we stay open till about three. That just about catches everybody. Still, we have our regulars who come through every year on vacation. They still stop. They have a few more gray hairs and wrinkles, but we remember them. Don't think I've ever seen you two before, have I?"

"My first time," I replied.

"Mine too," Nikki said. "I read about your place in a book about old Route 66 and had to stop in and see it firsthand."

"Glad you did, and hope the two of you come again."

Unlikely, I thought. I figured Nikki would hang with me for the day and then be off on her own again. I'm not the type that offers a promising future, and my gut feel was that her radar had picked that up about a mile out of Galena.

"So back to your story," I said. "What happened to your parents?"

"They were killed in an automobile accident two years ago."

"I'm sorry."

"It was devastating. If not for my work, I think I would have gone crazy. It was the hardest experience of my life, even worse than losing the baby."

"You lost the baby?"

"It was all part of the nightmare. I lost the baby a month after I got married. I should have had the marriage annulled like my parents wanted, but he talked me into staying together."

"Maybe he wasn't as dumb as I thought."

"Oh, he was. He just liked the thought of having sex every night."

"Yeah, my first wife was the same way," I joked. Suddenly sensing that the self-revelation party might be coming my way, I said, "Let's go."

"Hey, not fair! You haven't told me your story."

"I haven't decided if I can trust you." I left a twenty for Norma and headed for the door.

Oklahoma

Journal — September 15: *I'm in trouble. How do I always manage to get myself into these situations? Actually, I know exactly how I get myself into them. The way a man's mind can rationalize almost any behavior is truly amazing. So what about Nikki? I like her. But I don't really want to like her. I'd like to not like her, but I don't want to not like her. I'd like to sleep with her. But I'd like to not want to sleep with her. Charles Williams thought purely platonic love made it possible for a man and woman to share a bed without a sexual thought. I wonder what was wrong with Williams.*

I made it out the door before Nikki could catch up with me.

"Hold on, partner," she called. "What's the hurry?"

"I sensed intimacy developing, and I had to flee," I replied.

"Okay. But you owe me a story at the next stop."

"It's a deal. By the way, what would you recommend as the next stop?"

"I was hoping to hitch a ride to Clinton," she said.

"Clinton? As in our former president?"

"Clinton, Oklahoma, you goofball!"

"And what is in Clinton?"

"The Route 66 Museum."

"Research, I assume?" I said.

"And fun, too, if you behave yourself," she said.

"Then by all means, let's go to Clinton!"

I started the Harley, and she climbed on behind me. As I pulled into the street, she gently put her arm over my shoulder and gave a small hug. "Thanks for the pie," she said.

We didn't talk much during the ninety miles from Sapulpa to Oklahoma City. I found out her last name was Taylor. She made jokes about the Reformation when she found out mine was Calvin. We were on the Turner Turnpike, and I kept the Harley at a pretty constant 90 mph. I decided to follow the route of the old highway through Oklahoma City in honor of my friend Bo

Mitchell — another of the Route 66 connections in my life. Bo had grown up in Oklahoma City. His dad, Dale, was a should-have-been Hall-of-Famer for the Cleveland Indians in the fifties. A lifetime batting average of .313 on a World Series club — yet the fact that he was the final batter to strike out in Don Larson's perfect game will have to stand as his primary claim to fame. Dale had grown up in Cloud Chief, Oklahoma, just twenty-five miles down the road from Clinton. At the height of its urban explosion, Cloud Chief boasted a population of sixty-three.

Bo himself had been a pretty fair athlete, playing AAA ball for the Cardinals' farm team. When my life unraveled, Bo was there for me. His own short-term disaster in the real-estate business had earned him a six-month stay at what he jokingly referred to as the "Gray Bar Hotel." The experience sensitized him to the fate of those whose lives have imploded. The week before I left for Chicago, Bo and I met for breakfast. He handed me a large envelope containing twenty crisp, new, one-hundred-dollar bills. "Just in case," he said. I told him if I made it anywhere near Cloud Chief I would stop and burn a candle in honor of his dad.

I would have gladly bypassed Oklahoma City if it hadn't been for Bo's memory and Nikki's desire to see the Oklahoma County Line Barbecue. One of the few remaining vestiges of the old highway, the restaurant was a favorite hangout of Pretty Boy Floyd and other bootleggers, gamblers, and painted ladies of the twenties. Today, the restaurant attracts their modern counterparts — investment bankers, stockbrokers, and executive secretaries. I stood by the bike and stretched while Nikki took a quick look inside. She came out writing notes on a small pad and smiling.

"Good stuff?" I asked.

"Yes," she said. "Lots of pictures from the Pretty Boy Floyd era." She finished writing and walked to the bike, sticking the small pad in the pocket of her leather jacket. I had to wonder if I would merit any notes on her pad and what they might say.

"Let's go," she said as she once again climbed on the bike.

"Yes ma'am," I said, cranking up the Harley.

At Oklahoma City, I-44 continues south while old Route 66 heads west, parallel to and at times replaced by I-40. We headed west on state highway 66 toward Bethany, home of Southern Nazarene University, where we were greeted with billboards proclaiming, "The Fear of the Lord is the Beginning of Wisdom." We stayed on the road until it crossed the South Canadian River and intersected I-40. Jumping on the Interstate, I twisted the throttle a bit higher for the ride to US 62 south. Nikki hung on tight.

It is seventeen scenic miles from I-40 to Binger on US 62. Through hills and woods and red-rock canyons, US 62 works its way south toward state highway 152. It seemed strange to think that, three hundred miles due north, this same road runs behind my boyhood house in Russell.

We entered Binger to huge signs announcing, "Binger — The Home of Johnny Bench." Nikki asked me who Johnny Bench was. I said, "He's the guy who invented the bench." She slugged me in the arm.

Outside of Binger, we headed west on Oklahoma 152. The scenic stretch rapidly gave way to what I most remember about Oklahoma — long stretches of flat, desolate land. The good news was that 152 was long and straight and had recently been resurfaced. Five miles out of Binger, the road was empty, and I again opened up the throttle. In twenty minutes we were at the intersection of State Highway 55. Another three minutes and we made the turn for Cloud Chief.

There are certain pieces of the American landscape that are desolate and depressing. Cloud Chief occupies such a space. The fact that one of the greatest ballplayers in the history of baseball came from this place is truly remarkable. The current population is twelve, and we didn't see one of them. I stopped the Harley at a dilapidated ball field.

"What are you doing?" Nikki asked.

"Something I told a friend I'd do," I responded vaguely.

I opened the saddlebag on the right side of the Harley and dug around for the candle I had put there. While Nikki looked on, I walked to where home plate had once been. I lit the candle. Looking skyward, I said, "Lord, if you're actually there and still listening, I'd like to say a prayer in memory of Dale Mitchell."

Sensing no response, I blew out the candle and dropped it at the imaginary plate. I walked back to the bike with Nikki looking at me in a puzzled manner.

"You are a very strange person," she said good-naturedly. She reached out and patted my arm. I smiled at her.

"Let's go to Clinton," I said.

"Let's," she agreed.

✵

We hit Clinton in the late afternoon. I thought it might be an awkward moment when it came time to ask Nikki what we should do for the night. She preempted me by suggesting we get a motel room with two beds and share the cost. I said it sounded like a good idea. I knew it wasn't a good idea. Women might actually believe you can pull something like this off, but it will drive a man crazy — that is, if the woman sharing your room looks like Nikki.

I checked us in at the Trade Winds Courtyard Inn. Nikki told me to ask for room 215. The desk clerk smiled and said, "The Elvis Suite." I asked what he meant, and he explained that Elvis had stayed here a number of times and always took room 215. Nikki, I assumed, was doing more research. I handed the clerk my credit card. Nikki walked to the room while I went to move the Harley. I pulled it around the motel's swimming pool and right up to the door of room 215. Nikki was inside, checking it out.

"Let's go to the museum before it closes," she said.

I unstrapped her bag and handed it to her. Then I grabbed the bag liners that served as my packing system from inside each of the saddlebags. We left our jackets and gear with Elvis, splashed some water on our faces, and headed off.

The Oklahoma Route 66 Museum opened on Saturday, September 23, 1995. It sits on the outskirts of Clinton, right on Route 66. The Oklahoma State Historical Society built the museum with funding partially provided by a federal grant for highway enhancement. The local citizens also kicked in a quarter of a million bucks to make it happen. Although there are other museums dedicated to Route 66 in other states, this is by far the largest, and it is filled with the most extensive collection of authentic memorabilia.

I could tell Nikki was in her element. She again made notes on her small pad as we took a quick trip through the place. It was also obvious to me that *she* was the most popular exhibit in the place for fans of the male gender. She looked great in her faded 501's and red T-shirt. I hadn't noticed her belt before. It was dark brown leather, highlighted by what appeared to be genuine silver conchos, each imbedded with pieces of turquoise. Her western boots perfectly matched the belt. She was a very classy lady, even in her once-in-a-lifetime hitchhiking outfit.

"This is really great!" she said, walking across the recreated fifties diner that serves as the centerpiece of the museum. "They close in ten minutes but open early in the morning."

It suddenly hit me that a major decision awaited us. Was I going to spend a day in Clinton? Were we heading further West together? Would Nikki even want to spend another day on the back of the Harley? And the big question — what were we getting into tonight?

It had been a long, hot afternoon in western Oklahoma. The cool of the motel room felt good as I crashed on one of the two beds.

"Do you have a swimsuit with you?" she asked.

"Sure. Why?"

"I'm steaming, and the pool outside looks inviting. I thought I'd go for a swim. Want to join me?"

How could I say no to an invitation like this? "That sounds great!"

"You change out here," she said. "I'll change in there." She took her bag and disappeared into the bathroom.

I dug through one of the bag liners and pulled out my swimsuit. It took me less than a minute to kick off my boots and get out of my jeans and shirt. Pulling on my trunks, I noticed a gray hair on my chest and momentarily thought about the state of my aging body.

The bathroom door opened and for one moment, my heart stopped beating. "What's the matter?" Nikki asked with concern as our eyes met.

"Nothing," I replied. "I hope you won't think I'm being inappropriate, but you look great."

"I thought you loved me for my mind," she teased.

"That too." I tried to regain my composure.

She wore a small, but modest, white two-piece swimming suit. Every exposed part of her anatomy was toned like a well-tuned athlete's. I would have pegged her at 115 pounds distributed perfectly. In the white suit, with a healthy tan, the overall visual impression is hard to describe. Whatever you are imagining, I assure you, it is inadequate.

"Come on," she called as she walked out the door.

After an hour at the pool, I was ready for dinner. I had been sitting on a chaise lounge by the side of the pool while Nikki kept swimming lap after lap. I finally stuck my feet in the water at the end of her lane and got her attention.

"Whew! This is great!" she said as she stood up in the shallow end in front of me and tossed her hair back in one of those TV shampoo commercial kind of moves. I concentrated with all my mental energy so that I didn't stutter when I spoke.

"Want to get some dinner?" I asked, without mispronouncing a single word.

"Sounds great," she said. "I know just the spot."

"Another roadside attraction, as Tom Robbins might say?"

"You like him too?"

"One of my favorites."

"There's a classic Route 66 place called Pop Hicks Restaurant that I'd like to see."

"Nothing but the finest gourmet dining when you hang with me," I said.

❋

Pop Hicks was a true classic. The minute we walked in the door I felt as if I had been transported to 1962. Someone had done a marvelous job of maintaining the bona-fide Route 66 atmosphere. We grabbed a table by the window, and I looked around, noticing that everyone in the restaurant was looking our way and smiling. At first I thought they had probably seen us ride up on the Harley and were looking because of the bike. Then I remembered Nikki. No question about it — everyone was looking at her, and probably me, also. Her because of how great she looked — me because they wondered what the heck a guy like me was doing with a woman like her.

"You're a hit," I said.

She looked up and smiled. "I think it's the bike."

"Right!"

"Is this place great, or what!" she said.

"It's very cool. Good call."

"Let's order. I'm starving."

Nikki ordered the country-fried steak with green beans and mashed potatoes. I ordered a salad and a bowl of vegetable soup.

"How do you do it?" I asked.

"What?"

"Eat like you do and still look like you do. You know I've seen what's under those duds," I reminded her.

"I never eat like this," she answered matter-of-factly.

"Oh, this is part of the hitchhiking, picking-up-old-men thing?"

"I figured if I was going to do research, I'd go all the way. I usually stay on a pretty strict diet and workout regimen. But I have to confess to the occasional pizza-and-beer binge."

"I, on the other hand, am on the pizza-and-beer diet, combined with the G. K. Chesterton exercise program," I said.

"I'm familiar with Chesterton," she said, "but I never knew he had an exercise plan."

"Oh yes," I said. "He said that whenever he had the urge to exercise, he would lie down until it went away."

"Cute," she said. Then she switched gears on me — she looked me in the eye and said, "Okay, it's your turn."

"My turn for what?"

"You've heard my story; now I want to hear yours."

"It's not pretty," I said.

She didn't say anything. She bent forward and put her mouth on the straw of her drink without ever taking her eyes off mine.

"Okay," I said. I tried to figure out where to start.

"Five years ago my life disintegrated," I began. "Actually, I should probably say it self-destructed, or I destroyed it. At the time I had a pretty normal life. Actually, I had an above-average life — way above average, I'd have to say. I had been married to the same woman for almost twenty years. I had two children — I guess I should say I *have* two children. I had a successful career, and I lived in a nice home in suburbia with a dog, a cat, three cars, and a motorcycle.

"I worked hard at being a good husband and good dad. The fact that I came from a pretty dysfunctional family, and that my own internal issues were a constant source of stress, made the scenario I have just described extremely difficult for me."

"It sounds like you were doing a pretty good job, " she said.

"I'm sure everybody thought so. But in retrospect, I was a time bomb waiting to go off."

"In what way?"

"I had made a questionable decision regarding a career," I said. "I don't think I was really wired to do what I had been attempting to do for over twenty years. It took its toll."

"What were you doing?" she asked.

"I was a Presbyterian minister," I replied.

Nikki continued the focused eye contact. I am always aware of how telling someone you are a minister can suddenly change the entire atmosphere of a conversation. On airplanes, the revelation can often assure you of a peaceful, uninterrupted flight. Nikki's expression didn't seem to alter one bit. After a few seconds, she prompted, "And that made you a time bomb?"

"That and the circumstances surrounding my life," I answered. "I guess you could say that I didn't play well with a lot of the other guys who had made the same career choice."

"So you're in a job that doesn't fit, surrounded by a bunch of guys you don't like. Sounds relatively common to me. Not usually the material of blowups."

"The church was big," I said. "I was in a pretty desirable position. Looking back, I think there was a lot of envy involved. There are some pretty big egos in the contemporary church scene in the good old USA."

"How's that?" she asked.

"I think certain parts of the religious community in America are just as caught up in the pursuit of success as any secular corporation."

"Not exactly the poverty and humility of St. Francis," she said.

"I bought into that pursuit of success pretty heavily myself. In retrospect, I think my own emotional poverty made me horribly vulnerable. I have an unproven theory that more than a few of the people who go into the ministry are, at best, subconsciously motivated by similar dysfunctions. Personally, I found myself always needing more and more external validation. Nothing was ever enough.

"Over time, the inner pressure and outer tension became overwhelming. I was constantly stressed out at work, and to be honest, home was pretty stressful, too."

"I'll bet you were a great dad but struggled with the marriage," Nikki said.

"I don't know about that. It kind of went back and forth. Sometimes the marriage was the stressor, sometimes the kids. Why did you guess the marriage?"

"It's a pattern I see all the time. Dysfunction breeds dysfunction. Generally, you end up with a single parent — usually the mother — and a fatherless home. When Dad sticks around because of the kids, the marriage is often a bit of a sham, without intimacy or satisfaction." She had put on her PhD cap. It went pretty well with the rest of her outfit.

"Ours wasn't like that," I said. "We worked hard for a lot of years to keep it together. I think it was more the combination of professional stress and kids and my own internal struggle."

"What happened?"

"I became the object of some pretty nasty slander. I confronted the responsible parties. They denied it and used my confrontation as another point of attack. It just kept getting worse."

"These were other clergymen?"

"Like I said, the church attracts the best and the worst of humanity."

"I have to tell you — this still doesn't sound like the kind of material blowups are made of."

"It probably wouldn't have been if it hadn't been for what happened at Trail West."

"What is Trail West?" she asked.

"Let me set the stage for you. Trail West Lodge sits at the base of the Collegiate Peaks outside of Buena Vista, Colorado. It's a beautiful spot. We had quite a few of our denominational meetings there. I used to love driving there from Denver on highway 285. You start by winding up through the foothills outside of Denver, and in minutes you find yourself driving through incredible mountain scenery with long, winding roads and small mountain towns.

"On the occasion of my . . . what shall I call it . . . incident, I had to go to Trail West for one of the quarterly meetings I regularly attended with my colleagues. I had to miss the first evening session because of a previous commitment, so I woke up early the next morning and headed out of Denver at about five to get there by seven. At the time I had an old 911 Targa that I had restored. I was having a ball, keeping the Porsche at a pretty constant eighty-five through the turns heading up into the mountains. Then came Kenosha Pass and the long, flat plains of South Park.

"I came over the pass and dropped down into South Park just as the sun was breaking over the mountains in the east. I know you'll probably think I'm overdramatizing, but I'd been listening to some old Beatles tunes on CD. Just as the sun broke, "Good Morning" off the *Sgt. Pepper's* album started to play. I pulled over at the bottom of the pass and took the top off the Targa. Then I jumped back in the car, cranked up the sound, and blew across South Park at 120 mph. It was what I would call a peak experience."

"Sounds fun!" she said.

"It was. But the minute I arrived at Trail West the fun ended. I knew something was wrong immediately. Everybody was acting strange. You know — no eye contact — not sure what to say — weird. It didn't take long to find out what was going on. One of my friends pulled me aside and told me what had happened the night before. Two of the men I was having problems with had verbally attacked me in front of the entire group. I had been accused of being a prima donna, a constant self-promoter. They also made insinuations about the misuse of funds.

"I dropped my bags and asked where they were. I was not letting this pass. My buddy warned me to chill, but I couldn't. I walked down to the room where the meetings were being held. Both of the jerks were there.

"When they saw me, their expressions changed into a kind of self-satisfied smirk. I confronted them about what I'd heard. One went into a lame explanation about how they were only concerned for the good of the church and how I needed to 'get out of the flesh.'"

"What does that mean?" she asked.

"It's a theological concept, roughly synonymous with being a total ass."

"Oh."

"When he said it, something inside snapped. It was as if all the years of playing some kind of game, and taking all the abuse I'd taken in the name of religion, and all the grief these guys had been giving me, and all the stress of my home life, and all the dysfunction of my youth coalesced in a single instant — and I lost it."

"What did you do?" she asked.

"I hit the guy who said it in the face as hard as I could while screaming something about him being the kind of person who would engage in carnal knowledge with his mother. After that, it's all a blank. In court, the witnesses — "

"Wait a minute — what court?"

"I was arrested for felony assault and attempted murder."

"You have got to be kidding!"

"I'm told I followed the nose shot with a well-placed kick in the groin that resulted in him assuming a position something like a human accordion. But only for a minute, because my next punch was an uppercut that caught him under the chin and straightened him like a bolt of lightning had hit him. I'm told I continued to scream a running commentary on his lineage and sexual habits while throwing off anyone who tried to restrain me. Apparently, the last thing I did was throw him through a plate-glass window. When all was done, he spent a week in intensive care, and I spent three weeks in the Buena Vista jail, gradually coming to the realization that my life as a Presbyterian minister and model family man was probably over."

"Unbelievable! How long ago was this?"

"Five years ago next month," I answered.

Sometime during my story, the waitress had delivered our food. The food might have been excellent, but we would not have known it. Neither of us ate a bite. Nikki was engrossed in every detail of the story.

"How about if we get out of here?" I suggested.

"Good idea," she said. "I'm really not hungry anyway."

It was a beautiful night. We got on the Harley and headed out of Clinton on Route 66. The night air was turning cool, but the heat absorbed by the road during the day radiated upward and kept riding conditions comfortable, even without a jacket. Nikki kept her chin near my right ear, but we both kept quiet, enjoying the peaceful evening motorcycle ride. When 66 intersected Oklahoma highway 73, we turned and headed toward Foss Lake State Park.

We cruised around the northern end of the lake until we found a quiet beach area without a single camper. I pulled in and turned off the Harley. We walked down to the lakeshore and sat down. The sun had already set, but the remaining traces of day in the sky cast a spectral light over the lake. The cicadas were out in force, and the first few fireflies began to twinkle. Nikki moved close enough that our shoulders were touching. We sat quietly looking out over the lake. After a few minutes, Nikki spoke. "So you left me in Buena Vista with you in jail. What happened next?"

"I came to my senses in jail. At least I thought at the time that I had come to my senses. The offended parties had managed to convince the judge that I was dangerous to myself and to society and should be kept off the street. After three weeks, my lawyer did some fancy footwork and had me moved to the Arapahoe County jail, near my home in Denver."

"Didn't your family bail you out?"

"They tried. I wouldn't let them. I didn't want to see or talk to anyone. My lawyer tried to force them to kick me out, but it seems that if an American wants to stay in jail instead of getting bailed out, he still has the right to do so."

"What did you tell your wife and kids?"

"Nothing. I refused to see them. I'm telling you, something snapped. I went silent. I wouldn't even talk to the judge under oath. I sat there staring straight ahead. She didn't know whether to hold me in contempt or send me to the nuthouse."

"So what did she do?"

"My wife sat in court weeping, and my kids just sat stunned, unable to comprehend what had happened to Dad. Anyway, a couple of my friends convinced the judge that I really had flipped and needed medical help. I was sent to the regional mental health hospital and kept in lockdown for the next two weeks. It took that long for me to get to the point where I would communicate and cooperate. By that time, I realized that if I didn't cooperate, they could keep me locked up for a long time."

"How long were you in the hospital?" she asked. I could see I hadn't scared her off yet. I considered this a good sign.

"I was a resident at the mental health center for several more weeks. By the end of that time, I had devised what seemed like a completely rational plan. I decided to leave my wife, rent a small apartment, and start a new life. I would have had to quit my job except that I had already been fired and given six months' severance pay to help me 'pursue my giftedness elsewhere.'

"I was functional, but still loony as a jaybird. Ironically, the shrink who had been assigned to my case found my current state of mind much 'healthier' than the 'repressed style of existence that had led to the nervous collapse.' I was released, given the provision that I did outpatient therapy twice a week as stipulated in my sentencing hearing."

"How did your wife handle all this?" Nikki asked. Her expression showed that she had genuine concern for what had happened — and probably wondered what state my state was currently in, other than Oklahoma.

"She was devastated and angry. I could handle that. It was the kids that ripped me up."

"How did they deal with it?"

"Stephanie just got angry. She wouldn't look at me or talk to me. Teddy was too young to understand, but as long as I took him for a few days each week, he seemed to be okay."

"What did you do?"

"I applied for disability. Fortunately, the church carried a pretty good policy. I had the checks made out to Elizabeth and sent to her monthly to get her through the transition. I sold the house and split the equity. Then I got a job."

"Doing what?"

"Washing dishes. It really sucked."

"Then what?"

"I quit washing dishes."

"And?"

"It isn't very pretty."

"I want to know."

"I moved into a loft and had a series of relationships with other women."

"Brother!"

"I know. Stupid."

"Then what?"

"My wife moved to New Mexico with the kids." I answered with the precision the questions were being fired at me.

"And you?"

"I bought a lot in the mountains and an Airstream trailer."

"And?"

"I had one final affair with my ex-best friend's ex-wife and became celibate."

"Celibate?" I had just dropped the bomb. It was out of my mouth before I realized it.

"Oh, brother," I said. "I don't know how to explain it except that every time I got involved with a woman, it seemed to end in disaster, so I decided to become temporarily celibate."

"Let's come back to that later," she said. "So you were living in an Airstream trailer in the mountains?"

"For a while."

"Then what?"

"Then I took the Airstream on the road. I drove and thought

and took odd jobs to eat and pay for gas. I began to sort through what was crazy and what made sense and what I really believed and what I couldn't believe any more. I began to think that the heart of what I had believed was pretty sound, but something had gotten radically wacked in the way it had been worked out."

"Meaning?" she asked.

"Meaning, I knew I couldn't deny the existence of God without violating my intellectual integrity."

"But?"

"But I couldn't escape the fact that the way I had been living out that reality had put me over the edge."

"So?"

"So I started trying to figure out what a new life might look like."

"And?"

"And I got this crazy idea to take a trip on old Route 66 to see if I could pull it all together."

"This trip?" she asked.

"Yep. I thought maybe I could find some answers — plot a strategy — change course," I said, looking out across the lake.

We sat quietly as Nikki processed my story. After a few minutes she put her arm through mine and pulled me closer. I turned to look at her. She looked into my eyes, then closed hers as she delivered a long, passionate kiss.

"What did I do to deserve that?"

"You picked me up," was the answer.

"I should kiss *you* for that," I said.

"I think you should," she said, as she leaned into me again.

I drew her close. I kissed her gently.

We sat in silence until she asked, "What's next?"

"On the trip?"

"Yes."

"The original idea was to ride from Chicago to LA, making a few stops along the way. I spent some time tapping into my old network before I left, getting the names of a few people who supposedly have put the pieces together in a way that works."

"What do you mean?" Nikki asked.

"I think there are actually folks out there who have figured things out and are living like human beings were intended to live. I have the names of a half-dozen men and women who somebody who knows somebody who heard what I was doing thought I ought to stop and visit. I've spent time with a retired seminary professor outside of Chicago, a retired English professor in St. Louis, and a former minister in the boonies of southern Missouri."

"Any insight yet?"

"I'm not sure."

"Not sure?"

"You know all the stuff I told you about trying to conquer the world?"

"You mean your career and family?" she asked.

"At least the career part."

"Yes."

"According to their theory, I made what they call my ascent, and ended up with a false self-identity. Then I entered into the crisis stage. Supposedly, I'm somewhere in the middle of it," I said.

Nikki didn't say anything. She obviously was giving all I said a great deal of thought.

"Let's go," was all she finally said.

❀

Nikki was quiet on the ride home. When I asked if anything was wrong, she told me she was just thinking about what I had said. When I asked her what she thought, she just said that she thought it was all very sad, and then she got quiet again. I decided to enjoy the wind in my face and the beauty of the night.

When we returned to Elvis's room, Nikki grabbed her bag and headed for the bathroom to get ready for bed. I took off my boots, jeans, and shirt and slipped into the bed farthest from the bathroom, thinking I'd give her the closer bed.

Nikki came out of the bathroom wearing a simple white, sleeveless T-shirt and a pair of men's boxers. She walked past her bed and sat down on the end of mine.

"Are you okay?" It was the only thing I could think to ask as my heart kicked into an irregular rhythm.

"No," was all she said.

I sat up and looked her in the eye. Then I reached out and pulled her to me and held her.

"Could we sleep together tonight?" she asked.

As I started to object, she said, "Not sexually."

"I'm not sure . . . " I started to say, but before I could finish the sentence she kissed me on the nose, then on the cheek, then on the eyelid, and finally lightly on the lips. I kissed her forehead and lay back down, her head resting on my chest. I fell asleep dreaming of Galadriel. She was coming toward me out of the darkness. A light shone around her, and in her hand she held a vial filled with a healing potion.

In the morning I awoke from a restless sleep to find myself alone in the bed. Sometime in the night, Nikki had left. She wasn't in hers either, although the sheets showed that she had slept there.

Great! I thought. *Once again, the woman leaves without so much as a good-bye.*

Then I saw the note: "Swimming laps." No sooner had I read the note than I heard a key in the door, and Nikki came in, drying herself from her swim.

"Good morning, sleepyhead," she said as she dried her hair.

"What time is it?" I asked.

"Nine-thirty. Get dressed. We're going to breakfast and deciding what happens next."

"Yes ma'am," I replied compliantly.

She grabbed her bag and headed for the bathroom while I slipped on my jeans and ran my fingers through my hair. *Good enough for a day on the bike,* I thought.

We both ordered oatmeal, whole-wheat toast, and fresh-squeezed juice at Pop Hicks. She had tea, and I had coffee. Over breakfast we talked about our respective needs.

"You probably want to know if I'll go to LA with you, don't you?" she asked.

"Yes," I confessed.

"I can't," she said. "I have to stay here for a few days and do research. I also need to get back to Chicago next week for some personal business."

"It was a long shot," I said, disappointed.

"I'd like to make a suggestion." She had obviously been thinking this one over.

"Shoot," I said, taking a drink of coffee.

"I'd like to see you again. I think I'd like to know what, if anything, you discover on the rest of your trip. I also think that you better not pick up any more hitchhikers."

"Jealous?" I joked.

"No. We haven't known each other long enough for that," she said. "I think you need to avoid all unnecessary distraction."

"Are you just a distraction?" I asked.

"I don't think so. I think I might be part of the answer to your puzzle," she said seriously. "I don't say that lightly or flippantly. If I went with you, then I *would* be a distraction. I'd like to see you pursue your strategy with focused passion and get whatever is driving you nuts figured out. Then I'd like to meet again, somewhere."

"Seriously?" I asked.

"Seriously," she said. "I have only two requests."

"Shoot," I said.

"I have a friend in Albuquerque that I would like you to visit," she said.

"No problem," I replied.

"He's a Catholic priest," she said waiting to see how I would respond. I didn't. "I think he might understand some of what you're going through and be of some help. He's an old family friend, and I trust him immensely. Would you promise me that you will stop and try to see him?"

I thought for a minute. As a Presbyterian minister, I hadn't had many good experiences with Catholic priests, but I hadn't yet encountered one as a degenerate biker.

"I promise."

She handed me a piece of paper with a name, address, and phone number.

"What else?"

"Promise that if you put the pieces together, you'll come to Chicago," she said.

I thought for a moment. What I said next had serious consequences. I didn't want to shut the door on this relationship. Finally, I said, "I think you can do much better than me. You're in the prime of life and as beautiful as any woman on the planet. You can have any man you want."

"I might want you," she said. "But I would want all of you. I want the pieces you've lost and the pieces you haven't yet found."

I stirred my coffee and thought for a minute before I said, "I promise you two things."

"Shoot," she said.

"I promise that if I can make sense out of things and I find what I'm looking for, I'll be on the first plane to Chicago so fast it will make your head spin." Her expression told me I had said the right thing.

"But I also promise this. If I come to the end of the road and I'm as much of a mess as I am at this moment, you'll never hear from me again."

6

Texas

Journal — September 16: Today I'm leaving Nikki behind in Clinton. I do so with mixed feelings. I think she is right about the need to focus. So I'm off to see a priest! I wonder what my old congregation would think if they knew I was going to a Catholic priest for help. I've always thought that God must have a sense of humor. How ironic if a priest ended up being the one who helped me figure out how all this fits together. At the moment, I'm more concerned with making it for an entire day without female distraction. And just as important, how quick can I get across Texas!

I reluctantly bid Nikki farewell at the Route 66 Museum. I entertained the idea that a better man might have stayed.

My plan was to get across Texas as fast as I could. I would spend the night in Amarillo and head into New Mexico the following morning. I had intended to stop in Albuquerque anyway to see my son and ex, but now I also needed to get in touch with one Father Michael Flaherty and honor my promise to Nikki.

I alternated between riding the old highway and hopping up on I-40 when Route 66 was in disrepair. The western Oklahoma terrain was rolling and hilly for a good stretch out of Clinton. The land was studded with yucca and prickly pear as it slowly made its descent into the Texas panhandle. It took a little over an hour to get to Texola and the Oklahoma/Texas border.

By the time I hit the exit for Shamrock, Texas, Route 66 had all but disappeared. Across the panhandle the interstate was built virtually right over the old road. It was so straight and flat by this point that it looked like a monstrous airport runway. The sky had clouded up and looked like it might let loose a whopper of a thunderstorm. I was thirsty, so I pulled off the road and into a Texaco station to gas up and get a cold drink. Inside, I greeted the scraggly looking attendant.

"Nice bike," he said, through a few missing teeth and the vocal distortion caused by the wad of chewing tobacco in his cheek.

"Thanks," I said. "Heard anything about the weather?"

"Which way you headed?" he asked as he proceeded to propel a large wad of tobacco-chewing by-product into a bucket behind the counter.

"Toward Amarillo."

"You might get a bit wet," he said. "We've been having some big boomers in the afternoons. Big hail."

"Great," I expressed my dismay. "Hail hurts! I better get going." I paid for my gas and the Coke I had polished off and headed for the bike.

"You take care out there," my gas station buddy said with a big toothless grin.

I pulled out of the station and headed down the on-ramp, noticing that the sky was getting darker. I wondered if I could get to Amarillo before the storm hit when the first drops began to fall. Within a mile, the sky opened up and dumped. These are the times when I am grateful that the interstate system includes a multitude of wonderful overpasses that provide welcome shelter for vulnerable travelers like myself. The rain had started to turn to hail as I pulled under the McLean overpass. I parked the bike and looked for a good spot to lie down and wait out the storm.

Digging through my saddlebags I pulled out *The Way of a Pilgrim*. I found a relatively clean spot on the inclined concrete wall of the underpass and rolled my jacket into a makeshift pillow. I opened the book at random and began to read. On page twenty-nine, the pilgrim tells the story of meeting a captain from the Czar's army. The captain invites the pilgrim to join him on the road. They come to an inn where the two share a meal, and the captain tells the pilgrim his story.

When he was a young officer, the captain had a drinking problem that nearly ruined his life. One day, he was given a copy of the four gospels by a monk and told to read it whenever he had the urge to drink. His response reminded me too much of how I had treated the book I was now reading:

> I do not recall what I gave the monk when I took the copy of the Gospels from him, but I placed the book in my trunk with my other belongings and forgot about it.

A blast from a car horn distracted me. I looked up just in time to see a battered old blue Ford station wagon go by with a small girl and boy waving at me with their faces pressed against the back window of the car. I waved back and returned to my reading:

> Some time later a strong desire for drink took hold of me and I opened the trunk to get some money and run to the tavern.

There, staring the captain in the face, was the book. He began to read the gospel of Matthew. By the time he'd finished a couple of chapters, it was too late to hit the bar. When he woke up the next morning, he had another craving to drink, and so he decided to read another chapter of the gospel to see what would happen. As he read, the desire to drink vanished. The captain finally tells the pilgrim:

> By the time I finished reading all four Gospels, the compulsion for drink had disappeared completely.

Then came the punch line: The captain had been reading an entire gospel every night for the previous twenty years and had never had another drink! The captain and the pilgrim then stayed up till two in the morning reading the gospel of Mark together.

Russia, at the time of the pilgrim's journey, must have been a better environment in which to cultivate spiritual authenticity than the one I inhabit. Had the pilgrim and the captain been alive today, they might have abandoned the gospel and opted for watching *The Sopranos* on the inn's TV set. Spiritual disciplines had less competition in those days. I decided to practice the one Leppick had assigned me.

"Lord Jesus Christ, have mercy on me."

I used to pray quite a bit. In the past, I might have also prayed that the Source of all cosmic love, peace, and grace would move the weather front a few miles so that I could make it to Amarillo without incurring a hail-induced concussion. I wasn't sure anymore whether whatever or whoever was at the other end of the line gave a rip about such things, much less my own little existential crisis. It had been comforting to think that *YHWH*, in all his infinite power and concern, cared about every hair left on my aging head. If I was totally honest, I still had some small, irrational spark of belief that he might. It was a mystery to me. I couldn't go back. I didn't know how to move forward.

Waiting for the rain to break, I began going through the mental exercise of sorting out what I couldn't deny from that which I could no longer embrace. It was an exercise I had been through repeatedly in the last five years without much resolution.

First, I thought, *Is there a God?* I have processed all the data thoroughly enough to tentatively affirm this one.

Does he care? I hope so. I think so.

How in the world did I get to this place? I have created my own bed in Sheol.

But if he or she or it is sovereign and omnipotent, couldn't he have kept me from going over the edge? This has been where my sorting process usually breaks down.

An eighteen-wheeler blew through the underpass blasting his horn and shaking me out of my contemplation. The driver gave me a thumbs-up. I waved and returned to my reflections.

Someone once told me that most people do not have an intellectual problem with God, they have a moral problem, disguised as an intellectual problem. I think I have both.

So I pondered. If there could be a God, how can I know anything about him or her or it? I used to depend on the Bible as an authoritative source. If it is accurate, I have no ability to know a thing about God that he does not choose to make known to me. In other words, with all due respect to the efforts of the medieval scholastics, rational attempts to reason the existence of God are futile.

What happens if you throw out the Bible? You're left with other options in written form: the *Koran*, the *Gita*, the *Book of Mormon*, the *Tibetan Book of the Dead*, the *Celestine Prophecy*, and the complete, annotated script from the *Star Wars* trilogy. If not the Bible, then surely not one of these! I'd studied them all, and they were either inconsistent or full of little blue guys with flutes, or written by some control freak that claimed spiritual enlightenment to gain power, money, and sex.

If not in written form, then subjective experience rules and defines the transcendent. In which case, anything goes. Images of Shirley Maclaine come to mind, along with Larry, Moe, and Curly Joe. I would always have trouble accepting someone else's experience as the norm for authenticity.

If not objective authority, and not subjective experience, then what? "Thus saith the Lord." These guys were either wired to the source or mad as hell. I needed a breakthrough.

While I had been reading, the weather had been deteriorating. It was hailing hard now. Hail to the left, hail to the right, a solitary biker protected from the elements by the god of the overpass. A cool breeze blew through. I leaned back against my jacket and closed my eyes.

❋

DREAM SEQUENCE THREE:

The wedding party is getting a bit out of control. I can tell they are making the bride nervous. I'm beginning to feel nervous myself. I've forgotten to wear socks. Or did I intentionally not wear socks? I can't remember. The church is very strange. There is no back wall to the sanctuary. Instead, cliffs drop to the ocean below. The groomsmen have already taken their places and keep throwing things out the back of the church and over the cliff. The bridesmaids are looking worried as the guys keep getting more and more out of control. The bride is a mess, and her mom is not a happy camper. I have this sense that I'm supposed to bring some order to the chaos, but I don't have a clue what to do. No sooner do I step up on the platform to begin the ceremony than one of the groomsmen throws another groomsman off the platform and over the cliff into the ocean. Things really start to go bonkers.

The next thing I know, I'm up in the balcony with my shrink looking down at the chaos. He turns and says, "It looks quite a bit like your psyche."

Suddenly I'm back on the platform. The bride is in tears.

"Don't marry this guy," I advise.

"Can't you do something?" asks the mother-of-the-bride.

"Yep!" I say. "I quit!"

⊛

An air horn awakened me from my nap. Weird dream! The rain had stopped, and the sun was breaking through the clouds. I decided to head down the road to Amarillo.

Those who love riding the back roads of America have called the interstate a "passionless slab of monotony." The stretch from the McLean overpass to Amarillo could not have been more passionless. I twisted the throttle on the Harley and pressed hard toward my destination through the limitless emptiness of the scrub-brush-filled Texas countryside. On to Amarillo! The only "real city" in the panhandle, as the locals claim.

I exited the interstate on Amarillo Boulevard. Old Route 66 follows this street, and the feel of the past has been well preserved. Signs even boast that this was where "the Old West lingers on." Even though parts of the historic district looked pretty good, I couldn't find a motel that looked inviting, so I headed back out to the interstate and decided I'd have to give in and spend the night at the Big Texan. I'd been seeing signs for it ever since I crossed the Texas border. I thought I might even jump in the Texas-shaped pool before deciding whether I would attempt to consume the 72-ounce steak that came with a promise of being free if one could finish it in an hour.

"Hey there! Welcome to Big Texan!" My waitress had arrived. Dressed in western apparel, her petite figure was accented by the tiny size of her waist, circled with one of those western belts with a buckle the size of a stop sign. Auburn hair hung from her cowboy hat. Her nametag said "Ashley."

"Hi, little darlin'," I said. I used my best Sam Elliot impersonation.

"Is that your black Harley out there?" she asked.

"Yep."

"I love Harleys!" she said.

"Me too," I said. I tried to match her level of enthusiasm.

"My Daddy used to give me rides on the back of his."

"I've done the same with my little girl." The thought of this brought a slight emotional twinge. It had been a long time since I'd seen Stephanie, much less had her hold me tight while we cruised down some mountain road on a motorcycle.

"What can I get you?"

"How about a Lone Star to start with, and then I think I'll have the catch of the day."

"Sure you don't want to tackle the Big Texan? I bet you could eat a horse after a day on that bike!" She had obviously been trained to hawk the obscene cut of beef to every unwary stranger that wandered into the Big Texan.

"I'm allergic to beef," I lied.

"Bummer!" She walked away shaking her head as if the thought of a Harley rider who didn't eat beef had created a disgusting sense of confusion.

I was well into my trout and my second Lone Star when the boys came over to the table. Big in all directions, with wads of chewing tobacco sticking in their jaws, I was hoping they were not hostile.

"That your black hog out there?" the smaller of the three asked.

"Yep," I answered without looking up from the fish, and without the pseudo-Texan accent. I uttered a sub-vocal prayer, "Oh Lord, not again."

"Road King, ain't it?"

"Yep," I answered, looking up and evaluating the situation a bit more. I was relieved to see there appeared to be no malice on their faces.

"I been thinking about tradin' my Softail on one and thought I'd ask your opinion, if you don't mind me interruptin' your supper," he said with a genuine apologetic tone.

"Not at all. Have a seat, if you like." The three immediately took me up on my offer. "I hope you won't think I'm rude if I keep eating, I hate cold fish."

"Go ahead," said Texan Number Two.

"So how is the Road King? And by the way, I couldn't tell whether you're injected or carbureted," he said, showing some knowledge of Harley technology.

"I like it a lot. And it's the injected model," I replied, taking a pull on the Lone Star. "I'd offer to buy you a beer, but you're obviously well taken care of," I said, tipping my head toward the bottles in their hands.

"Thanks, appreciate that," said Number Three, in a good-natured Texas accent.

"Ever had a Softail?" Number One asked.

"Several," I answered.

"How does the Road King compare?"

"Smoother and more comfortable. I've never liked the styling quite as much, but for the road, I could never go back to the frame-mounted engine."

"I've got one of the '93 Nostalgias, which I hate to get rid of, but I'd sure like to have something like yours for the road. We went all the way to Sturgis this year, and I think I might have sustained permanent kidney damage," he joked.

"I had one of the Nostalgias too," I said. "That would be hard to give up."

"I took all that cowhide junk off and put on a normal seat and bags. It made a lot of difference in the way it looks."

"Me too," I affirmed his decision.

"Well, we'll leave you in peace to eat your supper. I just wanted to know what you thought. Keep that rubber side down, partner."

"Thanks, you too."

About the time the boys left, Ashley returned.

"How's the fish?" she asked.

"As good as the finest restaurants in Europe," I said. I had intended it only as a generic compliment, but I had pushed one of Ashley's buttons.

"Europe! I've always wanted to go to Europe! Have you been there?"

"I used to go there frequently."

"Ever been to Paris?" she asked excitedly.

"Um hmm."

"What's it like?'

"Old."

"And?"

"Lots of beautiful buildings. Lots of great food. Lots of great art and a lot of unhappy people."

"You're kidding!" she responded incredulously.

"It's actually a dreary place unless you have a great deal of money and are passionately in love."

"Did you, and were you?"

"Once I did and wasn't, and once I was and didn't, and several times I wasn't and didn't."

She looked perplexed as she walked away.

When she returned to check on me she asked, "How about London?"

"Oh yeah. Been there, done that."

"What's it like?"

"Old."

"Come on, you know what I mean. Isn't it extremely cool?"

"Cold, actually," I said. I could tell she was getting irritated, so I said, "It's old and beautiful, with a lot of great old buildings, and fair-to-mediocre food. The people speak a reasonable variation of English, and most of them are unhappy."

"So what does it take to be happy in London?" she asked.

"Money, a great lover, and an excellent umbrella," I said.

I could tell I was annoying her. She seemed locked onto the idea that somewhere out there a European city existed that might provide deliverance from life in Amarillo. I didn't have the heart to tell her that life in virtually any city in Europe was probably preferable to life in Amarillo. Why build false hopes?

"Is there anywhere in Europe where people are happy?" she asked.

"Amsterdam," I replied after a bit of reflection.

"What's it like?"

"Old."

She punched me hard in the arm. It reminded me of Nikki.

"It is," I said. "It's old and cold in the winter. And there are a lot of great old buildings and great old art and a few happy people."

"I don't get it," she said. "I thought Europe was totally cool. How can there be so many unhappy people?"

"Cool is not always happy. Actually, it has been my observation that what we think is cool is often an attempt at external validation that comes from deep insecurity and unhappiness."

"I don't have a clue what you just said," she said. She walked away shaking her head.

After dinner I headed back to my room at the Big Texan. It was early enough to do a little reading, so I thought I would return to *The Way of a Pilgrim*. Early in the story, the pilgrim meets a spiritual director who teaches him the Jesus Prayer. The teacher tells the pilgrim to try to pray the prayer three thousand times a day! The pilgrim gets very serious about the practice. He prays the prayer for hours a day and begins to get some benefit from it. He goes back to his mentor and tells him things are going pretty well. In response, the mentor tells him to pick up the pace and shoot for six thousand times a day! It takes the pilgrim ten days to hit this level. The teacher then comes to visit him and gives his new instructions:

> You are now accustomed to the Prayer, so continue with this good habit and strengthen it. Do not waste any time but decide, with the help of God, to recite the Prayer twelve thousand times a day. Rise earlier and retire later; stay alone, and every two weeks come to me for direction.

I had always been cautioned about the "vain repetition" prayers used by certain segments of the Christian world. What the pilgrim was practicing could easily be taken as such, except that he began to sense a rhythm to the prayer that synchronized with his heartbeat. He was also extremely sincere. What could be so bad about seeking mercy thousands of times a day? I could certainly use it. Unfortunately, every time I thought about praying, I was thrown back into my faith dilemma. For instance, how would God be able to give the pilgrim mercy and communion when he hasn't been able to spare the pilgrim's family or even his ability to make a living? It seemed incongruous, which is how it had seemed to me for the past five years.

I figured that by the time the pilgrim hit the twelve thousand mark, he would indeed be praying without ceasing. I also figured that approach would put a bit of a crimp in a normal pilgrim's social life.

When the pilgrim told his teacher that at times he feared he was praying mechanically, without meaning or feeling, I could relate. His mentor told him it didn't matter, just as Leppick told me. He went on to explain that the discipline was intended only to "kick start" the interior prayer of the heart — a foreign concept to me. The pilgrim had enough humility to buy that explanation and to keep praying until he established some kind of a cosmic connection that seemed to fulfill his quest. I didn't think that would be the way for me, but I decided I might need to step up the Jesus Prayer thing.

There is an attractive simplicity to the spirituality of *The Way of a Pilgrim*. Read a gospel a day and pray without ceasing. My own fall from grace had not been so much a lack of belief as an inability to live out what I said I believed, and yet the pace of the life I had created for myself often kept me from these simple disciplines. I'm sure this is what Leppick was thinking when he gave me the book.

I looked closely at my copy. It was quite wonderful. The old leather binding was still intact; the faded pages were all in excellent condition. It was a book collector's delight. *Thank you, kind Professor. I will treat it well, and when I have finished, I will make sure it finds a good and proper home where it will be well cared for.*

I turned off the light and decided I would Jesus Prayer myself to sleep, instead of counting sheep. *Tomorrow I hit New Mexico. I will see Elizabeth and Teddy. I will need all the mercy I can get.*

New Mexico

Journal — September 17: Today I reach Albuquerque. I get to see Teddy. I have to see Elizabeth. This has been the most painful part of my self-destruction: the wounds I have inflicted on my wife and children. I was never equipped to be a husband and a father. Maybe no one is. Where does all this fit into the male journey? Does Teddy need to be initiated? I am not able to do it. He has no community of men to teach him. Monroe said that when we do not initiate our boys, life eventually does. That was certainly true in my case, and look where it got me. I need some help here. If God is around, this sure would be a good time for him to show up.

The ride from Amarillo to the New Mexico border was relatively uneventful, except for a brief stop at the Cadillac Ranch. We are talking Stonehenge à la 1950s heavy metal here. If you aren't familiar with the phenomenon, picture a row of ten old, graffiti-covered Cadillacs "planted" side by side, nose down, at about a thirty-degree angle — supposedly the same angle as the Cheops pyramid. The sculpture was the brainchild of Stanley Marsh III, a millionaire who owns the field where it stands. I'm thinking someday I might plant a car in front of my house.

From the border of New Mexico to Edgewood, I rode in a kind of preoccupied daze, thinking about how I never know what to say or how to act around Elizabeth. My leaving devastated her. It wasn't her fault. I guess it's pretty hard not to take it personally when your partner of twenty years announces he doesn't intend to live with you any longer.

The town of Edgewood, New Mexico, sits thirty miles east of Albuquerque on old Route 66. In 1906, Joe Hill arrived here by covered wagon to homestead 1,280 acres that became the Hill farm. There was always some dispute whether Joe arrived by covered wagon or by train. As it turns out, it was both. He came by train from Tennessee to check out the available land. Emptying his pockets at the railway station, he asked for a ticket as far west as the money would get him. He made it to Moriarty, New Mexico, where he left the train and hiked west to the first available land. Having staked his claim, he returned to Tennessee, packed up his belongings, and headed west with his mother, via covered wagon.

In 1914, Joe married Mae Madole. They farmed the land and raised eight children. Number eight was a boy named Kenneth. Like his enterprising father, Kenneth became a shrewd businessman, parlaying his early real-estate holdings into an impressive portfolio and building what at the time was the largest real-estate company in Albuquerque. Kenneth met Maxine Hutchinson, a local beauty, married her, and had three children of his own. The youngest was a lithe and wispy reed of a girl named Elizabeth. She grew into a beauty herself and made the questionable decision of saying yes to my proposal of marriage.

We had two children. Our daughter, Stephanie, is now twenty and married to an engineer named Jed. I wasn't invited to the wedding. Our son, Teddy, moved to Albuquerque with his mother when I officially moved out of our house. He is now eleven and the greatest joy in my confusing existence. He is also my primary motivation to get my act together. He needs a full-time dad, and I want it to be me.

Joe and Mae Hill were well entrenched on their farm when the newly formed Interstate Highway Commission decided to run US 66 right through Edgewood. The year was 1937, and Albuquerque had a booming population of 35,000. It was already a self-sufficient community with deep Hispanic roots, but the position it held on the journey west and the popularity of the new highway running right down Central Avenue would launch a growth spurt that transformed the city forever. The replacement of the old road with Interstate 40 might have changed things along Central, but it only enhanced Albuquerque's position and accessibility.

I decided not to stop in Edgewood and look up any of the in-laws. The only one still speaking to me was Leslie, and I had made that promise to Nikki to avoid distraction. Leslie was Elizabeth's cousin and a definite distraction possibility. She was running the bed-and-breakfast old Aunt Alta Mae had built as an eccentricity. I stayed there a few years ago, and Leslie and I stayed up way too late and drank way too much tequila. Leslie was single and attractive and one heck of an artist. I kept going.

I took Interstate 40 to the first Central Avenue exit. Old Route 66 ran right down Central, and I had decided to stay at the Thunderbird Lodge — an old Route 66 classic. Further down Central I would run into the university area. My ex and son lived near the university in a little stucco house they had bought with the equity Elizabeth received out of the sale of our home in Denver. I checked in and took a quick dip in the pool before calling my son.

It was late afternoon when I finally reached Teddy. His voice reflected the excitement he always showed when we were able to spend time together.

"Hi, Dad. Where are you?"

"I'm down on Central at the Thunderbird Motel," I answered.

"Can I come down?" he asked, with the hopeful expectation a child has on Christmas morning before he opens his gifts.

"I thought I might take a quick shower and come pick you up on the Harley, if it's okay with your Mom."

"Cool!" he said. "I'll go get her."

As soon as Elizabeth came to the phone I experienced the same guilty feeling I had whenever I faced the past. She was cordial but cold, as usual.

"Hi, John."

"Hello, Liz. How are you?" I couldn't think of anything else to say.

"Pretty good, all things considered. I hear you've been on quite a trip."

"Did Teddy tell you?" I asked.

"He read me the e-mail you sent him before you left for Chicago." The technological revolution had helped me stay in touch with my son in a way I'm sure I never could have pulled off in the days of letter writing, stamps, mailboxes, and postal delivery.

"I've had an interesting trip," I said.

"I imagine you have." Elizabeth had that tone of "No kidding, you jerk," in her voice for the first time. I knew I'd better change the subject quick.

"Can I come pick him up?" I asked.

"I wouldn't dare say no."

"I'm down on Central at the Thunderbird."

"Oh boy, really living it up this trip," she said.

"I wanted to stick with the Route 66 theme."

"I'm surprised you didn't stay out with Leslie at Alta Mae's."

It was scary how well she knew me. "I'm trying to keep focused on the task at hand," I said.

"Which is?"

"I'll tell you some other time. I'll be over in about a half hour to get Teddy."

"Try to get him back at a reasonable hour."

"You know he'll want to stay with me. What do you think?"

"I guess it's all right. How long are you here for this time?"

"I don't know," I answered honestly, knowing my answer would not be well-received.

"I guess I should have expected that," she said.

Our interaction was deteriorating rapidly, so I decided to end it as quickly as I could.

"How about if he stays with me and I bring him home in the morning? I have a few things I have to do in town tomorrow that I don't think he'll want to do."

"I guess that will be okay." Her enthusiasm was overwhelming.

"Dad!" My son was back on the phone. "How long till you're here?"

"I'll be there in about a half hour," I assured him.

"Cool!"

I pulled out of the Thunderbird and headed down Central toward the University area. I like the laid-back feel of Albuquerque. I often thought we might have ended up living here or Santa Fe. Elizabeth and Teddy had.

It took about ten minutes to reach the house. It sits in a good neighborhood, and I felt a flash of gratitude that Elizabeth had been able to salvage a pretty nice life out of the rubble I'd created. The house was a small stucco built in typical New Mexico style. Large trees lined the street and shaded the houses. Most of the neighbors were students, professors, or young professionals who had chosen the ambiance of the city over the sterile atmosphere of the newer suburbs, ever spreading around the city like some malignancy.

Teddy heard the sound of the bike before I turned the corner. He stood in the driveway, my one-man greeting party. The sight of him generated the mixed feelings of joy and regret that time with him always produced.

"Dad!" Teddy yelled, arms waving like crazy.

I pulled into the driveway and shut off the bike. I'd hardly made it off before my son was hanging from my neck and almost putting me in need of Dr. Ali, my Persian-Wiseman-from-the-East chiropractor.

"Hey, son," I hugged him and gave him a big kiss on the cheek. I was grateful that he had not yet hit that stage where it is not cool to show affection for your parents.

"Dad! Dad!" he was so excited he could hardly get the words to match the speed of the thought. "Wait till you see what I built in the garage! It's a hovercraft that's about ten times more powerful than the one we did when I was in third grade. Max helped me with the engineering, and we got some of the coolest stuff at the flea market for so cheap you wouldn't believe it, and then I worked up the design on CAD, and Max took it to the lab, and the guys at the lab said we ought to send it up to Los Alamos because they thought that if I entered the science fair I might not only win at state but had a good chance to go to nationals and maybe win a scholarship, although I still want to go to the Air Force Academy if your friends will still help."

The velocity of the words was amazing. Nonstop ideas and rapid-fire speech had characterized Teddy since he was two. For the first two years of life he hadn't uttered a word. The doctors had been concerned that because of diminished hearing capacity, he might not have adequate ability to develop speech. After long months of evaluation for delayed speech development, he first spoke at twenty-four months. We had come down to New Mexico for the Balloon Fiesta. The huge, colorful balloons ascending over the Albuquerque plains had mesmerized Teddy.

In the car on the way home he was securely strapped in his car seat, sitting next to his sister. Without warning he said, "Fire makes the balloons go up." I nearly drove off the side of the highway. Not bad verbal and cognitive skills for a two-year-old. We knew then he was going to be something special.

"I can hardly wait," I interjected between breathing pauses.

"Dad, can I get my stuff and go to your hotel?" he asked.

"Sure, let's go get squared away and then grab something to eat."

"Not too much junk!" Elizabeth had come to the door to watch our reunion. She looked good. Her long, dark hair was pulled back in a ponytail that fell almost to her waist. Her jeans and embroidered work shirt showed that she had comfortably settled into the New Mexico vibe.

"Hi, babe!" It came out without even thinking, a reflex — something I didn't have the right to say anymore. Before she could respond, I added, "You look great."

"Thanks. You look like you've been on the road for a week."

"Yeah, I've got the old road look going."

"Max is coming in a few minutes, so I thought you might want to grab Teddy's things and get going," she suggested.

"You're still seeing Max, then. How's that going?" I asked, even though I didn't want to know the answer.

"It is going great," she said. There was an emphasis on the "going" that let me know her life without me was just fine.

"I guess he must still be at Sandia Labs, if what Teddy has just machine-gunned at me is accurate."

"He is still at Sandia," she offered without embellishment, for which I was grateful. I had already heard of how important his job was, and how much money he was making, and how he was an old flame of Elizabeth's from high school, and how he had asked her to marry him and move into his big pad. I knew a whole lot more about Max than I wanted to.

"Great," was all I could muster. Turning to Teddy, I said, "Let's grab your stuff and get out of here."

"Great idea, Dad!"

It was late afternoon as we headed out of the neighborhood. Teddy waved with pride at the neighbors who had come out to hear the source of the rumble that had disturbed their peace and quiet. It was too early for dinner, and Teddy wanted to go for a ride, so we hopped on I-25 and headed south out of town, getting off the interstate as quickly as possible and riding one of the back roads that surround Albuquerque. Teddy wore an open-faced helmet we had painted to look like Peter Fonda's in *Easy Rider*. It enabled him to keep a constant conversation targeted at my right ear. We headed back into town just as the sun was setting over the Jemez Mountains in a glorious blaze of orange, pink, and blue that only happens in New Mexico. Teddy would have picked McDonald's or Burger King for dinner but approved my suggestion of the Old Firehouse restaurant on Central.

Sitting across from him at the dinner table, I couldn't help but notice how much he had grown since I saw him last. A bit small, he was wiry and strong, a result of his passion for rock climbing. He had never liked the more popular sports, such as baseball or football, but had excelled at climbing since, at the age of five, he scaled the test wall at REI in about thirty seconds. I remember the look on the instructor's face as he turned to me and said, "A natural!" I had never climbed in my life, but that didn't stop Teddy. Unfortunately for me, and fortunately for Teddy, Max was an avid climber who had climbed his way into Teddy's heart, and maybe Elizabeth's bed.

"Why are you staring at me, Dad?" Teddy broke my reverie.

"You look like you've grown two inches since I saw you last."

"Actually one and three-eighths," he said. "Mom says it's another growth spurt. I had to get new jeans for school."

"Bummer," I said jokingly.

"Dad, I also need some new tennis shoes. Actually, I don't need them, but Nike has these new shoes that have this really cool shock absorption system, and Mom said they were too expensive, but if you wanted to buy them for me she would let you; what do you think?"

"Fortunately for you, I came into a bit of cash right before I started my trip."

"Royalties?" he asked. He had always gotten a big kick out of opening letters from my agent to see how big the checks were. Lately, they'd been getting smaller since I hadn't written anything in a while.

"No. Actually, an old friend gave me some dough. I think he was afraid I'd end up somewhere out in the desert, broke and busted down, and no one would ever hear from me again."

"Cool!" Teddy's response resounded with youthful enthusiasm. He smiled at me with an expression of admiration I no longer deserved.

"I guess I could spare a few bucks for the latest in high-tech footwear."

"Thanks, Dad. When can we go look at them?"

"How about tomorrow afternoon? I have something I have to do in the morning, and I promised your mom I'd have you home before I go."

"Tomorrow is Sunday," he said. "What do you have to do on Sunday morning?"

"I have to go to Mass," I said.

"Why?" he asked with a puzzled look. He knew I hadn't been in church much in recent years and that I'd never been a big fan of Catholicism.

"I promised a friend I'd look up a priest here," was all I said. I figured he didn't need to know more.

"Can I go with you?" His puzzlement had now turned to eagerness, as if going to Mass were a new adventure.

"It's fine with me if it's okay with your Mom," I said. "Are you guys going to church anywhere?"

"We hop around. Mostly we end up at some place Max goes. Mom says the theology is weak — but look where good theology got us anyway. That's what she says. I don't agree, but I read the Bible and pray on my own, so church isn't that big of a deal."

I wish I could figure out my own spirituality as simply as he had. Jesus did say that you need to become like a child. Maybe this was what he meant.

"So where are we going to Mass?" he asked.

"Something called the Center for Spiritual Formation and Action."

"Sounds kind of weird," Teddy said.

"Let's hope so!"

The Center for Spiritual Formation and Action wasn't actually a church. When I called to find out the time of the services, the guy on the other end laughed. I finally found out that Father Michael was speaking at a small Hispanic church down near the Rio Grande. After a gourmet breakfast at the Route 66 Diner, Teddy and I headed toward the valley and St. Theresa's church.

The Catholic Church had always been an enigma to me. They either seemed so rigid and liturgical that I came out feeling like I'd been at traffic court instead of church, or so loose the only thing I recognized was the bread and the cup. St. Theresa's leaned in the latter direction, and with Father Michael speaking, he pretty much pushed it over the edge.

The congregation was mostly Hispanic, but a healthy bunch of Anglos had shown up, like myself, to hear Michael. It seemed he was something of a celebrity in this neck of the Catholic woods. He was speaking on coming to grips with our brokenness, a subject I could relate to, if not in a theological way, at least experientially. His text was Paul's famous struggle of Romans 7: the old, "I do what I don't want to do, and don't do what I want" passage.

I don't remember everything he said, but I loved his summary. He ended his sermon by concluding, "The basic message of this text, and the period in Paul's life it reflects, is that sooner or later we all need to look at ourselves in the mirror and realize, 'I'm just a big jerk, and I need all the help I can get!'"

After the service, Teddy and I went to the front of the church and introduced ourselves.

"I've been expecting you," Michael said.

"Really?" I asked.

"Nicole called," he said.

"She made me promise I would get together with you," I explained.

"She's a sharp lady," he said.

"She never explained what your connection was to her."

"I knew her when she was a young girl in Chicago. I spoke at her family's parish a few times. I had this wild youth ministry in Chicago. We were young and idealistic and unrealistic, but a lot of families in the Catholic Church wanted to send their kids to us in those days. When Nicole hit her adolescent rebellion, her folks called and asked me to come and see her. Anyway, I helped her through some tough stuff."

"She's a remarkable woman," I said.

"Well, I don't know what you did, but you sure impressed her."

"I picked her up hitchhiking," I said.

"You've got to be kidding! Hitchhiking?"

"She said she had never done it before and would never do it again, but she stuck out her thumb in Galena, Kansas, and mine was the first piece of machinery to come along. I'm not usually looking for hitchhikers, but in her case . . . "

"What are you talking about, Dad?" Teddy broke in.

"Someone I met on the road made me promise to come and see Father Michael here," I answered. "Father—"

"My friends call me Chip," he interrupted.

"Chip, this is my son Teddy. He lives here in Albuquerque with my former wife."

"Nice to meet you," he said, extending his hand to Teddy.

"Nice meeting you, too," Teddy responded, with a lack of enthusiasm that probably made Flaherty wonder how sincere he was. Teddy's shyness came across as aloofness—another inherited trait.

"Would you like to get together tomorrow?" he asked.

"That would be great," I replied. "I'd like to figure out where you go after you've discovered you need all the help you can get."

"It's a pretty heavy theological concept, but I'm just the guy who can help you figure that out," he joked.

"Nine o'clock at your office?" I asked.

"I'll look forward to it."

We shook hands and moved away so the others who were waiting could talk to him.

❀

The Center for Spiritual Formation and Action was located in an old Catholic school on the fringes of downtown Albuquerque. No sooner had I pulled up in front of the operation than about twenty little Indian kids surrounded my motorcycle. I might have been hijacked had it not been for Michael's intervention.

"Okay. Back inside, you little red ankle-biters," Michael teased. As the raiding party broke up and headed back into the building, he turned and said, "So much for political correctness."

"You sure command immediate response," I marveled.

"You obviously have not been on the receiving end of a Jesuit yardstick," he joked.

"Hardly. I come out of the Presbyterian, cognitive-reasoning approach to child development."

"À la Spock of the sixties?" he asked.

"À la Princeton in the seventies."

"Didn't work, did it?"

"Nope."

"Come on in," he said.

We walked into the building and down the hall to a door marked "Office." Inside, a group of women sat behind a counter much like the one I'd dreaded in high school. The only difference between then and now was the upbeat atmosphere that seemed to permeate this operation.

"Sisters," Michael said, "meet the esteemed Reverend Doctor Calvin."

The women all looked up from their desks and conversations to wave and mumble greetings.

"Where did you come up with that introduction?" I asked.

"Nicole filled me in on who you are and why she wanted you to see me."

"Since she never told me why she wanted me to see you, perhaps you can fill me in." We walked into what I assumed was his office.

"It seems that our young friend thinks you and I have a great deal in common, except that your vow of chastity had a different motivation than mine, and I am not wandering the country on a motorcycle."

"And if you were not a priest she would have seduced you years ago?" I joked as we sat down facing each other.

"If I were not a priest I assure you she would not have had to seduce me. She would have had to chase me away. And you, my friend, are some kind of a lucky object of transference of her girlish crush from years past; only you have the good fortune of being able to do something about it."

"Not till I get some things sorted out," I said.

"So I'm told. I'm supposed to expedite that process and send you back to Chicago," Flaherty said with one eyebrow cocked, carefully scrutinizing me.

"And what makes you think you have the capability of straightening out a bent and relapsed Presbyterian?" I asked.

"Well, thanks to Vatican II, at least I don't have to try to convince you to join the one, true, Mother church."

"I do feel kind of strange talking to a priest about this. It feels too much like confession."

"You Protestants are all alike," he said good-naturedly.

I wasn't sure what he meant by that but decided not to pursue it. Looking around the room, I was surprised how spartan it was. I thought back to the luxury of my own offices before my exit from the ministry. The contrast was unsettling. Half of the administrative operation of the Center could have fit into the sitting area of my executive suite.

"I know something about your blowup, or burnout. At least I have Nicole's version. She also said you had been doing some work on the male journey. Tell me about that," Michael said.

"I'm supposed to be praying the Jesus Prayer and reading *The Way of a Pilgrim*."

"That's it?"

"I've also met with three wise, older men who tried to help me figure out my struggle," I said.

"Three wise men?" he said jokingly. "What did they have to say?"

"They'd all had some experience with a kind of roadmap of the male journey."

"A map?" Michael said.

"More a kind of diagram that shows the stages guys are

supposed to go through. According to them, my 'crisis' is right on schedule."

"What does that mean?" he asked.

"They all seem to think that men in our culture spend the first half of their lives pursuing what they called *ascent* — a kind of upward mobility. Then somewhere around the midpoint of a man's life, the direction is supposed to change to a kind of *descent,* or downward mobility. The trigger for the descent is a time of crisis."

"The Great Defeat," Michael said.

"What's that?" I asked.

"Just a term some spiritual directors use for the midlife transition. What else did they teach you?" he asked.

"A little about faulty self-identity and how male initiation is supposed to prepare you for all this."

"It sounds like pretty solid spiritual formation stuff," he said. "Are you familiar with St. John of the Cross?"

"I know who he is — dark night of the soul and all that."

"It's pretty similar to your crisis-and-descent idea. He actually saw the dark night as having several stages. It was a time of what he referred to as purging."

"And that is . . . "

"Purging is a kind of descent. It's a process through which God deals with the falseness in our lives. You could picture it as a part of downward mobility standing in opposition to a cultural kind of success or upward movement," he said.

He had a whiteboard in his office, and I walked over to it and drew the diagram of the journey as I remembered it. My napkin had pretty much bit the dust in the rainstorm outside Amarillo. When I finished, I sat down. "This is the diagram they used," I said.

Michael took a few minutes looking at what I had drawn. "If I tried to fit St. John of the Cross into this, I would say that the descent needs to be divided into several stages," he said, moving to the board.

"St. John said purgation leads to illumination, and illumination to union." He divided the descent line into three parts. "Do you know what the crisis is intended to produce?"

"My understanding is that it is supposed to start you on the descent," I replied.

"True," he said. "But do you know what the descent is about?"

"Not really. I know it is supposed to be the opposite of the ascent, but I'm not really sure what that looks like.

"The ascent is a time when a man pursues what he perceives to be the life that will give him what he needs."

"I understand that," I said.

"Primarily, he gets his sense of dream or vision from the culture."

"I think I understand that, also," I said again.

"So if this dream is false, then at the midpoint it should begin to fall apart, right?"

"That's the idea," I said.

"And theoretically, this falling apart moves a man into the downward part of the journey."

"Correct."

"Then why is it that many men never get there?" he asked.

"What do you mean?"

"I mean, how many men do you know who are moving downward intentionally?"

"Not many."

"And why is that?" he asked.

"You tell me."

"When I am working with men, I teach that every man will reach one of three destinies," he said. "I can tie it into this diagram pretty easily." He drew two additional lines from the crisis part of the diagram. One went up, a continuation of the ascent line. The other, a broken line, went straight to the side.

"If you don't have a clue about what we are talking about," he continued, pointing to the top line, "and you live in America, it's probable that you will attempt to continue to ascend, even if you go through a crisis."

"I think I see more of that than the downward stuff," I said.

"This is the man who never 'gets it' in spiritual terms. He attempts to continue to ascend — and he pulls it off. Do you know what we call this man in America?" he asked.

"Successful?"

"Exactly! But this is the guy I call the Old Fool," he said. "I get that term from the guy Jesus talked about who kept building bigger barns. Remember him?" He wrote "Old Fool" above the ascending line.

"I know the parable."

"Jesus said that at the end, God calls this guy a fool."

"What's the middle line?" I asked.

"This is the guy who doesn't 'get it' and keeps *trying* to climb the ladder, but he doesn't have the ability to make it happen." He wrote "Bitter Old Man" at the end of the broken line. "He goes through crisis but doesn't understand what is happening, and his failure turns to bitterness. America is full of this kind of man. It's tragic."

"And what about the bottom line?" I asked. "What happens to the man who makes the descent?"

He wrote "Holy Fool" at the end of the descending line. "He becomes the Holy Fool," he said. "I take that from St. Francis. He called himself the 'Clown of God.' You could interpret the phrase as 'Holy Fool.'"

"And why would anyone want to end up down there?" I asked, pointing to the "Holy Fool" area.

"Because that is the place of reality," Michael said. "And whatever else God is, he is always reality. Let me walk you through it again. The wisdom journey takes you on the adventure of revealing and dealing with an illusion most men have embraced.

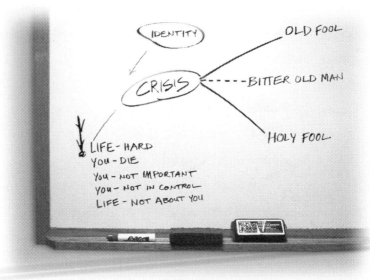

We call it 'success.' The man who has achieved it will have more problems than most men who have not. That is why Jesus said it is hard for a rich man to enter the kingdom of heaven. But it's more complicated than that. The man who does not achieve his dream, but never realizes it was the wrong dream, stays stuck in the illusion also."

The significance of the diagram began to take on more clarity as the thinking behind it emerged.

"This, then, is where the crisis comes in. It needs to shake you to the core. It can be a single event, or a series of incidents that last for years. God knows exactly what each of us needs. If you look at it this way, you begin to understand why sometimes what we think of as 'bad' things are actually 'good' things, and what

186

we think of as a 'good' thing might actually not be very helpful at all."

"I'm not sure I really understand all this," I confessed.

Michael turned and smiled at me. "That's good," he said.

"It is?"

"If you thought you had this all figured out, it would be a sure sign that you had no clue what it really means."

"Oh," I said, still not sure I either understood or bought what Flaherty was saying.

"There's a great deal of mystery in authentic spirituality, and most of it cannot be fathomed fully by cognition. It is heart material and hard to articulate. Also, the further down the wisdom journey you travel, the less certainty you will have about most things eternal.

"The wisdom journey is the process of coming to terms with what is real and important. It forces a man to confront the falseness in his life and shed the illusion. Ultimately, this is the man who can take a long hard look at the world and laugh at it. He understands the absurdity. In cultural terms, he becomes a fool. But in Kingdom realities, he is a Holy Fool, and that is a good thing. It is the goal of the male journey." He pointed at the words "Holy Fool." "Not many of these around."

"I don't suppose you are one of the few?" I asked.

"Nope. Not old enough," he replied with a smile as he sat down again.

"So how old do you need to be?" I asked.

"I don't think there are any set rules. But I have never met a man I would consider a true Holy Fool who was much younger than seventy."

"Seventy?" I said, astonished.

"Doesn't fit the cultural norm, does it?" Michael replied. "The Holy Fool is the biblical elder. The word *elder* means one who is old. Age was an asset in the Hebrew world. That's a foreign concept in America and the West, even in the church."

"I know what you mean," I said. "I became an 'elder' before I was thirty. In the Presbyterian system, the minister is technically ordained as a 'teaching elder.'"

"Doesn't make a lot of sense, does it?" Michael observed.

"So how does all this relate to me?" I asked.

"I'm not sure I can answer that," he said. "There are a great many possibilities. But I'll ask you one question."

"Shoot."

"Have you ever gone into solitude?"

"What do you mean?"

"How much time have you spent in solitude?"

"Five years," I said.

"I think not," he stated with that gentle yet authoritative tone he was so good at. "You are confusing aloneness with solitude. You've been alone and isolated for the last few years, but I doubt that you've experienced solitude."

"You'd better explain," I said. "I'm not sure what the difference is."

"If you read that little book that was given to you, you will notice the frequent references to the early Fathers."

"You mean the *Philokalia* stuff?"

"Exactly! It is the collected writings of some of the early hermits who went out to meet God in the desert. They lived in solitude. Solitude is intentional, and it is focused. You choose to be alone and undisturbed so that you can get in tune with God. It is a lost art in the West." Michael paused, smiled, and added, "Except in a few rare places like the desert of New Mexico."

"You specialize in solitude?" I asked.

"We provide some of the best solitude this side of the Egyptian desert."

"And you figure that I might get some answers to my questions?"

"I have no clue," he answered honestly. "But if you have the guts to try it, I have a place."

"So how long does it take?" I asked.

"A lifetime," he answered. "But two or three weeks will get you off to a pretty good start."

"Two or three weeks!" I exclaimed.

"What's wrong? You aren't one of those microwave Presbyterians who think all life's problems can be solved in a twenty-five minute sermon, are you?"

"I can't see myself sitting in the desert for a week."

"Unfortunately, most men can't. Think about it. If you get the inclination, give me a call, and we'll set something up."

I got on my bike and headed back to the motel. I liked Flaherty, but I couldn't see myself going off for a week on some screwball Catholic retreat. I felt confused and empty. I should have been used to the combination by now, but I still hated feeling like this. I decided to go back and swim some laps before picking Teddy up from school. I had to decide: Would I stay or head out again? I knew Teddy would want me to stay, but I also felt I needed to keep on my journey. In three days, I could be on Santa Monica Boulevard, and the final stretch of the highway.

I picked Teddy up from school and took him shopping for the tennis shoes he wanted. We found them at a mall that also had a movie theater, and we took in a flick. After the movie, he asked if we could go out for pizza. Elizabeth had decided not to let Teddy spend a second night at the motel and had given me till ten to get him home. We ate at a "gourmet" pizza joint on Central. It was a spectacular early fall night, with just a touch of chill in the air. Cruising down the street with my son's arms wrapped around me felt really good.

We arrived at the house at 9:45. Elizabeth came out to meet us and sent Teddy in to get ready for bed.

"See you tomorrow, Dad?" he asked as he headed inside.

"Unless I'm out in the desert," I answered. I had told him over dinner about my time with Father Flaherty, and he had decided that the desert thing sounded pretty good, if I could ride into town every night and take him to dinner.

"Don't go without me," he yelled as he walked out of my line of sight.

Elizabeth lingered on the porch after he went in. We shared an awkward moment before she spoke.

"He really needs you," she said. I could tell she was expressing more emotion than she wanted to show. "I've done my best, but a boy his age needs a dad. Now look at me." A lone tear trickled down her cheek.

I wanted to say something, but I knew I would probably say the wrong thing and make her feel even worse.

"I think I'll get a glass of wine. Would you like one?" she asked, trying to regain her composure. It was the first time in five years she had invited me to stick around.

"I'd love one," I said. She went inside to get the wine while I looked around the porch. There were two chairs and a table on what was actually a covered patio. The fact that it had been built in front of the house fit the New Mexico culture. It made sense to me. In front, you could enjoy your neighbors and the neighborhood. The typical back patio of most suburbs in America, with its fenced-in yard, further isolated you from your neighbors in what was already an isolated existence. Elizabeth's table had a large, well-used candle in the center. It looked as if this was a favorite nightspot for Elizabeth and, I guessed, my replacement. I decided to keep my mouth shut about it.

"Here you go," she said, coming out the patio door carrying two large glasses of wine. She handed me a glass of what looked and tasted like a Merlot. She sat down in the chair across from me with what had to be a Chardonnay. Five years had gone by, but we still had our predictable habits.

"How was your time with the priest?" she asked. I guessed that Teddy had filled her in on my trip to the Center for Spiritual Formation and Action.

I wasn't sure how to answer. I had been mulling over my time with Michael and had not yet reached my own conclusions. "Interesting," I decided to respond—a nebulous answer that could mean a lot of things. "He thinks I should go out in the desert for a few weeks and see if I have a spiritual experience of biblical magnitude."

"And what do you think?" she asked.

"I'm not sure. I think that given my present state of mind I might go crazy. Of course, that might be exactly what I need. Then again, if I went and nothing happened, it might further crush what little faith I have left." I figured my answer just about covered all the bases without being too committal.

"Are things any better?" she asked.

"I don't know," I answered. "I guess the fact that I'm on this trip is some kind of progress. A year ago I wouldn't have done it."

We sat silently for a few minutes, sipping our wine and enjoying the New Mexico night. After a not-so-awkward silence she dropped the bomb. "I think I'm going to marry Max," she said.

I didn't know what to say. I wasn't even sure how I felt. After the words sank in, I felt I needed to respond, since she sat looking at me, waiting for one. "I don't know what to say. Are you really in love with him?" A dumb question for an estranged husband to ask.

"Yes," she said hesitantly, as if her answer needed some qualification. "I love him in a different kind of way than I loved you."

The past tense was hard to hear, even though by now I should have just been glad that the anger had settled down enough to warrant a glass of wine and a civil conversation.

"It's not passionate, like we had in the early days," she continued. "I guess it's that over-forty kind of love — more companionship than a back-seat hormonal kind of love."

"Is that what we had?" I asked with a smile.

"At first, for sure," she smiled back. "Those were great days."

"I'm really sorry," I said without thinking. I had apologized a thousand times over the last five years, but never in such a friendly setting and never with more sincerity than I felt at the moment. She teared up again.

"I hate you so much for what you've done. It's really hard to forgive you. I watch Teddy come alive when you pull in the drive, and I know how sad he will be when you decide it's time to head out again."

I sat quietly. I had nothing to say. I had inflicted great pain in the lives of the three people I loved most. What can you say?

"When I finish the trip, maybe he could come stay with me for a while." She had full custody. I had never had Teddy for more than a few days, and Stephanie wouldn't come see me if I was on my deathbed.

"I'm not sure that would be a good idea, or even that I would let him. He's only eleven. Just a little boy."

"I guess I ought to see where I end up before I make any invitations that I can't keep anyway. I've let him down enough; I don't want to promise something I can't deliver."

"I think Max being here all the time would be good for him," she said. I took another sip of the wine as I thought about that idea. I hated the thought of someone else needing to fill the void I had created and desperately wanted to fill again.

"Maybe," I finally spoke. "I think what he really needs is for me to be here all the time."

"What do you think the realistic possibilities of that happening are?" I could tell she wanted an honest answer.

"I wish I could tell you. I can't go back to the way things were. I don't want to go on the way things are. I just can't find the place that works between the two. That's what I hoped I might figure out on the trip."

"Are you any closer than you were when you left Chicago?" A skeptical tone now colored the question.

I took a final drink from the glass as I carefully considered how to answer. "I'm not sure." I could see the disgusted expression return to her face. "I guess it's naive to think that a few days on the road will resolve things. I don't even know what to do with what I've experienced along the way." I didn't think it would be wise to go into details, especially about Nikki.

"Maybe you ought to go to the desert."

"Maybe you ought to marry Max and forget about me." I said it, but I immediately wished I could have taken the words back.

She stood and looked down at me. "Maybe you ought to go."

I stood. "Maybe you're right."

"Are you staying over tomorrow?" she asked.

"I'll see," was all I could answer.

"He'll be crushed if you leave," she said.

"I'll try," I said, heading for the bike.

I'm not sure how long I had been awake as the sky began to lighten. Long enough to realize that I was on the proverbial horns of a dilemma. I had been pacing back and forth across the room, trying to decide if I should stay or leave. Experiences like I'd had with Elizabeth tended to throw me into a very dark state of mind. I wanted to stick around for Teddy, but I also knew I had no idea how I could pull it off in a way that wouldn't push me back over the edge.

I didn't know what to do. What were my options? I could go to the desert and hope that God showed up and told me how to put my life back together. I could stay and try to be a father to my son. I could leave before anyone woke.

I knew I could not pull off most of those options, even if I wanted to — and at some level I wanted to more than anything I had ever wanted in all my life. I also knew that the one option I *could* pull off seemed heartless and cruel.

There are defining moments in all our lives. In a split second, or a minute at most, we have to decide, and our decision shapes the course of our life. Faithful husbands or wives allow themselves to get into a compromising situation, and the moment comes when either like Joseph they flee, or like Judas they sell out. There is that one moment when everything is on the line, and the decision is theirs, and they have complete freedom to choose. This felt like that kind of a moment.

I slipped on my jeans and boots. I thought of Elizabeth and

Teddy sleeping peacefully a few miles away. I could almost see his little body hanging over the edge of his small bed. I put on my shirt and jacket. I walked quietly out of the room and put my things back in the saddlebags. I turned the ignition of the Harley to the "on" position. I hit the starter button, and the bike roared to life. As I pulled out onto Central, I hoped that at least Elizabeth would let me say good-bye to him.

The streets were quiet as I pulled into their neighborhood and into the driveway of the house. Before I could make it to the door, Elizabeth opened it and came out onto the porch.

"I'm leaving," I said.

"You're such a jerk!" she said.

"I'd like to tell him good-bye."

"I bet you would," she said.

"Give me a break."

"You don't deserve one."

"Will you wake him up?" I asked.

"No," she said. "But don't worry. I'll cover for you. Not because you deserve it, but because he doesn't deserve to go through what he always goes through."

"I'll come back through on my way back from LA," I said.

"Don't bother," she said.

I got on the bike and quietly rolled it down the drive so that I would not wake him. Elizabeth had already gone back inside. I started the engine and headed out of the neighborhood. As I turned onto Central, I imagined Teddy standing on the porch. I could almost hear him call out, "Dad! Dad! Come back!" I looked in the mirror, and for a moment, I imagined seeing Elizabeth, standing on the porch with her arms around my son.

I took Central to Interstate 25 South. A mile south I took the I-40 West exit. "Lord Jesus, have mercy on me."

Arizona

Journal — September 19: *I feel about as low today as I ever have in the last five years. Something about being around Elizabeth makes me feel like I'm losing my mind. Sometimes I think Teddy would be better off if I just disappeared. I felt hopeful somehow after my time with Flaherty. If I read him accurately, there is a way. I don't know what it will take to get me where I need to be, and I have no idea how I will begin the wisdom journey instead of the embittered journey or the way of the Old Fool. I'm not sure I've ever met a Holy Fool. I guess Leppick and Monroe are about as close as it gets. As for me, I think I'm just a plain fool, nothing holy about it. I'm going to call Teddy. I hope he will forgive me . . . again.*

I had been on the road about four hours when the Harley began to sputter. I had crossed into Arizona, and there wasn't a promising stop in sight. I pulled over and got out my map to consider my options. The next intersection hooked into highway 191. On my map it was also marked US 666, which somehow seemed more appropriate. The fact that the road was identified as a scenic byway helped me make my decision. The nearest town on the route was St. Johns. St. John — the advocate of the grace of God. Maybe I could find a little grace in St. Johns, and maybe there would be a mechanic who could work on a Harley.

I nursed the bike down the road until I began to see some promising signs advertising both Fat Bobs Route 66 Service and Merl's Diner. If nothing else, at least I could take in a little middle-of-nowhere Arizona local color on Route 666.

I was feeling pretty depressed. My mental image of Teddy calling from the porch, the thought of what I just put Elizabeth through, again, and now the bike breaking down all combined to produce a sick feeling in my stomach. I didn't have the ability to process the conflicted feelings I was experiencing about the right thing to do — and how it differed from the choices I kept making. I was a mess. In other words, things were back to normal.

My existential wrestling match was interrupted and filed into some remote recess of the old gray matter by my first sight of the well-advertised diner and adjoining filling station. Sitting smack dab in the middle of nowhere was a meticulous-looking fifties-style diner and the most rundown, junk-laden, sign-plastered filling station I had ever seen. The visual contrast was stark. My hope was that someone at the service station could take instructions over the phone on the repair of sequential-port fuel injection and that, if necessary, FedEx could find this place before I went crazy.

I sputtered into the service station just as the Harley died. I got off the bike and turned to see someone who at first glance I figured had to be Fat Bob. I would have pegged him at about 5'11" and at least 250 pounds. With long, gray hair pulled into a ponytail and a huge, bushy white beard, he vaguely resembled Santa Claus in greasy overalls. I hate to describe his eyes as "twinkling," but it's the only word that accurately captures the effect.

"Oh yeah," he said, as he approached the bike while cleaning his hands on a shop towel. "Harley-Davidson Road King. Carbureted or fuel injected?" He asked.

"Fuel injected," I answered.

"Didn't sound too good pulling in," he observed.

"Something's off with the fuel system or the ignition. I've been sputtering along for about an hour now."

"Bummer!" he said, walking around the bike.

"Any chance you might have a look at it?"

"Sure," he replied with a confidence of which I was skeptical.

"Are you familiar with Harleys?"

"Familiar?" he chuckled. "I could take one apart and put it back together blindfolded. Have a '39 FL in the garage if you'd like to take a look. Merl has a new Ultra himself."

"Who's Merl?"

"My twin brother. He runs the diner," he said, pointing across the gravel lot at the diner.

"And I assume you're Bob?" I asked.

"Nope," he said, again with a chuckle. "Everybody assumes that, given the name of the station and the size of my waistline. I'm Jack."

"Who's Fat Bob, then?" I asked.

"What, not who," he replied.

"What?"

"That's right. What. I named the station after the 5.2-gallon Harley gas tanks."

"Fat Bobs," I acknowledged.

"Voila, Fat Bobs," he affirmed with his characteristic chuckle. "You did notice there was no apostrophe, didn't you?" Suddenly he became serious. "Now, what are we going to do with your hog?" He wasn't actually asking me—just talking to himself as he reached down and turned on the ignition switch. He walked around the bike and with the heel of his boot tapped the shifter until the neutral light came on. At this point, it at least appeared as if he knew what he was doing. Switching on the starter, he waited until the fuel injection light went out and then engaged the starter. The bike sputtered and coughed, but wouldn't fire.

"Well, something is definitely not right here," he said. "I'll tell you what, why don't you go over and grab a bite at Merl's, and I'll see if I can figure out what's going on."

"I sure would appreciate it," I said. I walked across the parking lot and up the steps of the diner. By the time I'd reached the door and looked back around, Jack had pushed the Harley into the garage bay and was already tearing away at it. Whatever skepticism I'd felt before was now progressing into the early stages of panic. What if this guy didn't have a clue what he was doing? It didn't seem like I had a lot of options, so I decided to get something to eat and hope for the best.

Unlike Fat Bobs, the diner was spotless. It also was pure, classic fifties, right down to the vintage Seaburg jukebox sitting inside the door and the remote selection boxes in each booth.

There were six booths along the front windows of the diner with seats covered in bright red Naugahyde. The tabletops appeared to be made of white Formica. The floor of the diner was covered in large black and white square tiles that glistened like an ad for Mr. Clean. Across from the booths stood a long counter with six chrome stools, also covered in red Naugahyde. Behind the counter, the top half of the wall opened to the kitchen, which was filled with stainless-steel kitchen appliances along with an amazing collection of shining cookware. All was spotless. Just as I was being caught up in the marvel of what I had found out in the middle of nowhere, the door to the kitchen swung open, and Merl entered.

I would have sworn that Jack had rushed around from the filling station, taken a quick shower, changed clothes, and now stood before me pretending to be Merl. They were nearly identical — same hair, same beard, same waistline, same glitter in the eyes — twin Santas! The only differences were in the minute features of their faces. "Hey there!" he greeted me.

"Hi."

"That your Harley I heard sputter into Fat Dubs?" he asked.

"That would be mine," I said.

"Didn't sound too good," Merl observed. "Sounded like a shot plug or a problem with carburetion."

"I think so, but it's fuel injected, not carbureted."

"So is my Ultra!" Here came the grin and twinkle.

"Your brother seems to think he can figure it out."

"No question! He's the best wrench this side of the Rockies."

I breathed a short sigh of relief. "Then I guess I'll have some lunch while he checks it out."

"That, my friend, is an excellent idea," Merl said.

I had a bowl of the soup of the day, a delicious chicken vegetable, obviously homemade, and a small dinner salad. I was the only customer in the place, so Merl and I carried on a conversation while I ate and he worked in the kitchen.

"This is an awesome diner," I said.

"Thanks," Merl said from the kitchen. "We're awfully proud of her."

"Do you mind me asking how you happened to end up out here?"

"It's a long story," Merl said, poking his head through the opening in the wall. "We had her shipped here all the way from New Jersey. Jack and I wanted to come out West, but not anywhere the crowds get too big."

"I think you accomplished that objective," I joked.

"Some folks might think this is a pretty stupid place to land, but Jack and I like being located on a blue highway, and we liked the ring of the name St. Johns."

Before I had a chance to respond, the door opened and Jack walked in.

"Hello, Brother Jack," Merl said.

"Hi, Bro," Jack said.

"Figure it out?" Merl asked.

"Yep."

"Is it good news or bad?" I asked.

"It's good news *and* bad news," Jack said. "What do you want first?"

"You decide," I said.

"Well, first of all, the problem isn't major."

"I guess that's the good news," I said.

"It's your injection system."

"That doesn't sound like such good news."

"Could be a lot worse," Jack said. "It looks like the chip in the computer has gone haywire on you. A new chip, and you should be on your way."

"Why do I have the sense that you're getting ready to give me the bad news?"

"The bad news is that there isn't a chip anywhere in a five-state region. It will have to come out of Milwaukee, then get shipped to the dealer in Phoenix, and then FedEx will have to bring it over here," Jack said.

"Let me guess the rest. It's Tuesday afternoon, and Milwaukee is already closed, and so it will be Wednesday before they can even order the part and Thursday or Friday before it gets here," I said.

"Actually, it could be Monday or Tuesday, given my past experience with the bunch that runs that place over in Phoenix," Jack said, without the grin, chuckle, or twinkle.

"Great." I said. "I guess I'd better find out if St. Johns has a motel," I said.

" 'Fraid not," Jack said.

"Where's the closest place to stay?" I asked.

"Back on the interstate, but you don't want to do that," Merl said.

"You could stay with us," Jack offered.

"Definitely," Merl agreed before I had a chance to comment.

"We have a guest room at our place, and we would love to have company," Jack said.

"We're just down the road a few miles, and you could have the place to yourself most of the day while we're working," Merl added.

I was reluctant, but such hospitality didn't come along every day. "How can I pass up an offer like that?" I said.

"You can't," they said in unison.

I spent the rest of the afternoon helping out at Fat Bobs while Jack tore into the fuel injection unit on the Harley. At six o'clock sharp, both the station and the diner shut down, and the three of us headed down the road in Merl's 1959 Jeep 4x4 pickup. I sat in the middle of the brothers and had the funny thought that I must look like the filling in some kind of Santa Claus sandwich.

We stayed on Highway 191 until we hit St. Johns, proper. The drive through town assured me that the decision to stay with the boys was a good one. On the far side of town, Merl steered the Jeep off the main road and onto a gravel county road that headed off to the west. About 500 feet down the road I spied a sign that read "Zion Reservoir — 10 miles." The road began to climb, and the scenery shifted to pine-covered rises and red-rock plateaus.

Five miles up the road, we turned onto an unmarked dirt road that headed farther up into the hills. It seemed that the brothers had chosen to live in seclusion.

The road wound through a pine forest that appeared to be virgin, except for the road running through it. We drove another twenty minutes until we broke through the trees onto a plateau that overlooked a large lake and panoramic views encompassing hundreds of miles. I figured the lake was Zion Reservoir. No sooner had we broken into the open than Merl took a sharp right onto a gravel drive that led into some pines for a few hundred feet. At the top of the drive, the woods opened onto the brother's home.

I don't know what I was expecting, but somewhere on the ride there I began to envision a one-room log cabin with dirt floors and outside plumbing. The only part I had right was the log part. The house was constructed of massive logs and built right into the side of a hill with a full view of the expansive scenery and the lake. It was a two-story affair with a large deck wrapped around three sides. The sharply pitched roof was covered in bright turquoise metal. Nearly the entire face of the house was glass. "Whoa!" I said.

The brothers looked at each other and smiled. "Just a little place to call home," Jack said.

"It's beautiful," I said, as he opened the door of the pickup, and we got out.

"Thanks," Merl said. "Took quite a few years to build, but we're proud of her. We lived in a little one-room cabin with dirt floors when we first moved to this part of the country. We were a lot tougher in those days."

"Younger, too!" Jack added.

"We used to come up here and sit for hours looking out over the lake. One day Jack said we ought to think about building a cabin up here. Most of the land off to the west belongs to the Zuni Nation. This area was mostly national forest land. One day we were buying groceries down in St. Johns and heard about a parcel an old fellow was selling that he had owned since the land-grant days. Ends up, it was right up here."

"We bought it all," Jack said. "We own most of the mountain, if you can call it that."

"You did a phenomenal job," I said as I admired the home.

"Thanks. We brought in a bunch of boys from back east that had been building log homes longer that you would believe," Jack said.

"Let's quit yakkin' and go in," Merl said. "I'm hungry as a horse. I've been cooking for everybody else all day, and I'd like to eat a bite myself."

The double doors on the lower level opened onto a set of doublewide wooden stairs that led up to the main floor. One step into the house and I was struck with the aroma of food cooking.

"I put a pot roast on timer when I left this morning," Merl said. "It ought to be ready right about now."

At the top of the stairs, the house opened into a massive greatroom that included the kitchen, dining area, and living room. At the center of the room, a circular fireplace divided the space into its various uses. The living room was adjacent to the wall of windows with the panoramic view that had first greeted us when we broke through the trees. The room vaulted a full two stories. On the opposite side of the room from the windows was a reading area. Two large, obviously well-used overstuffed leather chairs faced each other between the fireplace and the far wall, which contained a bookcase holding what must have been several hundred volumes of richly bound books. These guys were full of surprises.

Scanning the titles on the shelves, I discovered that every book was either a classic, written in some other language, or something I had never heard of. Nearly the entire center section of the wall was filled with works on philosophy and theology.

"Nice collection," I said, not knowing what to say.

"You'll notice a few by your namesake," Jack said. "In the original language."

Sure enough, right in front of me were a number of volumes of Calvin's Institutes in French. The leather looked very old.

"Have a look if you'd like," Merl invited.

"Maybe later," I said.

"I don't blame you. All I want to do is eat," Jack said.

"Give me a minute, and I'll have it ready," Merl said. "Why don't you take John Calvin here up to the loft."

"Good idea," Jack agreed.

To one side of the reading area, a set of steps led up to a room above the kitchen that looked out over the living and reading rooms. The large space contained a bed, more overstuffed chairs, a few tables with lamps, and a private bath. The decor was rustic and Adirondack in its feel. I knew I would enjoy the time I spent here. Even from the loft, you could see out the windows to the lake and beyond.

"Make yourself at home," Jack said. "We'll call you when supper's ready."

"Thanks," I said.

Jack went down the stairs. I turned and dropped backward onto the bed to catch a few minutes rest. My landing startled me. I sank so far into the mattress that it took a second to realize it was a feather bed. When I finally came to a stop, I felt like I was floating. This was the kind of bed you didn't want to get out of in the morning. I must have been lying down only a few minutes before I drifted off. The next thing I remember, one of the brothers was calling out, "Soup's on!"

The smell of dinner had filled the cabin. I don't know what Merl had done to that pot roast, but the aroma started my salivary glands flowing like Pavlov's pups. The table was set as if they were entertaining royalty. The bread looked fresh and homemade. The two brothers sat opposite each other and placed me at the head of the table. No sooner had we all sat down than Jack stood back up and picked up the loaf of bread. He lifted it above his head with both hands and closed his eyes. Merl's head was bowed as Jack began to pray.

He started in what was obviously Hebrew. I picked out the words *baruch* and *adonai*. Then he broke into English: "Blessed art Thou, O Lord, our God, for you have given us bread to eat. We give you thanks."

He picked up a glass of wine and, lifting it, began speaking in Hebrew again. He finished again in English: "We give you thanks for the fruit of the vine that you have given to make man's heart glad. Thank you, Father."

As Jack sat down, Merl said, "Amen!"

"Amen," I added.

The brothers both looked at me and smiled. Merl picked up an ornate tureen and began to dish out the pot roast. Jack poured wine from an unmarked bottle that looked suspiciously like the bottle I had enjoyed with Wolf in the Ozarks. I decided not to say anything. I thought I'd pitch in, so I took the bread and, looking to make sure I wasn't violating some unspoken order of things, began to slice three pieces off the loaf.

"We're glad you can be with us," Jack said.

"I feel a bit overwhelmed," I confessed.

"Why's that?" Merl asked, as he finished serving and picked up his knife and fork to dig into the meal.

"You're hospitality is so gracious. I don't feel I deserve it."

"Hospitality is not something you need to deserve," Jack said, bringing his glass to the center of the table to offer a toast. "It is a gift. To our new friend John," he said.

"Here, here," Merl added, then said, "I wouldn't be surprised if you haven't enjoyed quite a bit of hospitality over the last few days. Your trip sounds fascinating."

"I hadn't thought much about it, but you're right. My scheduled stops have been filled with terrific hospitality."

I took a sip of the dark red wine. It was fruity and robust in its bouquet. It was *exactly* like the Ozark wine. "This wine is wonderful. Where do you get it?" I asked.

"A friend of ours makes it," Merl answered. "He sends us a couple of cases every year."

I didn't ask. The rest of the meal was filled with jovial conversation. The brothers told me story after story of men and women who, like myself, for one reason or another had found themselves stranded in St. Johns. Some of the stories were hilarious. Others were heartbreaking. All had a bit of the mystical about them.

"How do you explain all these incidents?" I finally asked.

"Providence," Jack answered, without hesitation.

"Definitely," agreed Merl.

"What do you mean?"

"We believe people are led to our little refuge."

"Explain that to me."

"It's like this," Jack said, "You're heading down the road when something goes wrong with your car—"

"Or motorcycle," Merl added with a grin, looking me in the eye.

"Right," Jack went on, "And you look at a map or road sign for the nearest place to get some help and you see this funny sign about Fat Bobs, or Merl's Diner, and you think it's just coincidence that you happened to stop here."

"But it isn't?" I asked.

"What?" Jack asked in return.

"Coincidence?"

"No way, José. Providence. The Hidden Hand."

"And how do you know that?"

"It's why we're here."

"Of course it's why you're here," I said. "Why else build a gas station and diner, if not to fix broken cars and feed hungry people."

"Obviously, there is that. But what I mean is, we believe we were led here to fix *certain* cars and motorcycles and to feed *specific* hungry people."

214

"You're making it sound like the Twilight Zone."

"Actually, more like the X-files. The Truth *is* out there."

"So you're suggesting that it is part of the great cosmic plan that I broke down in St. Johns."

"You of all people ought to be open to that possibility," Merl said.

"What do you mean?"

"I mean, you're John Calvin on a spiritual journey, seeking the Truth. Aren't you? Why wouldn't God lead you to the place you needed to be to find it?"

"And I'm going to find it here?"

"Who knows? But if you do, Jack must be right. Don't you think?"

"To Truth!" Jack exclaimed with his glass lifted high.

"To Providence!" Merl added with great enthusiasm.

"To Santa!" I said, unable to help myself.

DREAM SEQUENCE FOUR:

I'm floating on a cloud while parts of motorcycles float all around me. There are mufflers, air cleaners, handlebars, ignition modules, frames, Fat Bobs; they are everywhere, like little angels in motorcycle heaven.

When I opened my eyes, I realized that I was floating on a cloud — sunk about a foot-and-a-half deep into the feather mattress. We had stayed up pretty late discussing providence, sovereignty, and other related issues. I hardly remembered staggering up the stairs to bed. I had some vague recollection of being carried up the stairs by one of the brothers, but I couldn't be sure.

It was a gorgeous day outside, and the changing colors of the leaves made the panoramic view from the cabin that much more spectacular.

I could smell coffee brewing, but there wasn't a sound in the cabin to indicate that the brothers were up. I climbed out of bed and headed for the stairs. I hadn't noticed before, but the cabin was so far removed from the white noise of civilization that the quiet had an eerie effect.

At the coffeepot, a note awaited me:

Gone to work. Have a relaxing day. Make yourself at home. There is a hiking trail down to the reservoir. Help yourself to whatever is in the fridge.

Both Jack and Merl had signed the note. I looked up at the clock. It was 12:30. I couldn't remember the last time I'd slept past noon. I poured a cup of coffee and looked around for a paper. Dumb move. There obviously was no delivery up here, and my hunch was that the brothers didn't care enough about the local news to get one at work. I hadn't noticed any paper machines at either the station or the diner. There were fresh croissants on the counter and what looked like homemade jam. I opened the refrigerator and took out a small pitcher of cream for the coffee. A dish of sliced fresh fruit was sitting in the fridge with a note that said, "Enjoy!"

I ate a croissant and the fruit while I slowly savored my coffee. I thought about turning on the television to see if I could get some news, then noticed there wasn't a television. There wasn't a radio either. There wasn't a phone. There wasn't a magazine. Only the books and the brothers in this place. There was a stereo system with a turntable and a CD player, but no appliances that hooked you up with the outside world.

I sat by the windows and drank another cup of coffee. It was the first time I had been alone and quiet in days. That wasn't always a good state for me. It wasn't long before my time in Albuquerque began to fill my mind. The memory of Teddy kept coming to the center of my consciousness. I hated these thoughts. This was when I really needed a television or newspaper to distract me. When all else fails, start moving.

I rinsed the dishes and put away the food. If I kept moving, I didn't have to think. The note caught my attention and enticed me to take a walk down to the water. I went up to my room and put on a pair of jeans and a sweatshirt. I put on my tennis shoes and grabbed my ball cap. Keep moving. Keep moving. Keep moving.

The trail to the water wound down through tall pines. The woods were dense and desperately quiet. About a half mile down the trail, I lost all sense of where I had come from, and the reservoir below still wasn't visible. The trail kept winding, down and down and down.

I had been walking for about a half hour when I heard the sound of a radio or stereo coming from up ahead. I came around a bend, and there was a small clearing off to my right with a campfire and a young man sitting on a log, smoking what appeared to be an illegal substance. The music was coming from a portable CD player; as I got closer, I could make out some kind of reggae/hip-hop/rap tune. He spotted me and nervously jumped to his feet.

"Whoa, dude! You scared the crap out of me!" he exclaimed.

"Sorry," I said. "I was hiking down to the lake."

The kid was wasted. His hair was a mass of knotted dreadlocks. He wore tattered jeans and an old plaid flannel shirt, worn open over a dirty thermal undershirt. He looked as if he had been living in the woods and hadn't taken a bath in some time. But the most disturbing part of his appearance was his eyes: bloodshot, glazed, and more than anything, empty. This was not a happy camper.

"Yeah, well, I was just trying to find a quiet place to smoke a little weed, man." There was something strange in his voice. I couldn't put my finger on it.

"I'll leave you alone," I said, starting to move on.

"No, man," he interrupted. "Don't go." Now there was a slight note of desperation in his voice.

I walked over to the fire. There was a sleeping bag rolled out near it and a duffel bag that probably contained all his worldly possessions.

"Want a cup of coffee?" he asked.

"Thanks, but I'm pretty coffeed out," I replied.

"How about some grass," he offered, holding out a joint.

"Thanks, but I gave that up about thirty years ago."

"I'd offer a drink, but I ran out this morning," he said, pointing to an empty bottle of Johnny Walker Red near the sleeping bag.

"How long have you been out here?" I asked.

"Just a couple of nights," he answered.

"How did you get out here?" I asked.

"We're just up the trail from the water. I've been hanging out in Arizona all summer — just drifting from park to park. That way you can always get a john and some water."

"It's going to start getting cold," I said.

"It won't matter," he replied in a downcast tone.

"What do you mean?"

"Last night was my last night."

"Here?" I asked.

"Anywhere," he said, as he reached to his side and pulled up a .357 magnum revolver. He pointed the gun straight at my face. Stark terror filled my universe. My life didn't pass in front of me, for which I was grateful, but a bizarre train of thoughts raced through my mind. I wondered what would happen to my motorcycle. I wondered who would take Teddy to get shoes next time. I tried to remember who I had made the current beneficiary on my insurance policy and if I still had one. It was all a quick rush of miscellaneous neurons firing with no apparent pattern except the sense that I was about to die. I was sure he would shoot me. I looked him straight in the eye, unable to say a word. Slowly, looking back at me with those empty eyes, he turned the gun toward himself, stuck the barrel in his mouth, and pulled the trigger.

I spent the rest of the afternoon in a state of shock, attempting to answer questions for which I had no answers. The police and paramedics were just leaving when the brothers got home from St. Johns. They had heard the news in town and shut down the station and diner early to come be with me. Sitting outside on the deck, Merl kept trying to feed me, and Jack kept filling my glass with homemade wine — two unique approaches to giving comfort.

"I don't get it," I said.

Merl and Jack sat quietly.

"What pushes a guy over the edge like that? He couldn't have been much more than twenty years old. Surely, that young, you don't get to a point where blowing your brains out is the only solution."

The brothers kept quiet. They sat with their heads hung, looking at the ground.

"The look in his eyes. It was so hopeless. It was like he had become an empty shell without a reason or will to go on. I don't get it."

The sun began to set behind the western plateau. It cast long rays of orange and crimson across the surface of the lake. The beauty of the scene stood in stark contrast to the horror I had witnessed only hours earlier. The gunshot had blown off the side of the drifter's head. Blood and brain matter had flown everywhere. Looking at the shattered mess on the ground, I had immediately thrown up. Now the images just kept coming back into my mind — the eyes, the gun, the shot, the blood, the lifeless body.

"It's not supposed to be like this," Merl said. They were the first words either of them had spoken in some time. I looked up and caught him staring at me.

"It's not supposed to be like this," he said again, now with a slight shaking of the head.

"Maybe we could have helped," Jack added. "I don't think he came through town or stopped. I would have remembered him." I could tell that Jack believed, if he could have got hold of this guy, things might have turned out differently.

"How could you have helped?" I asked. For some reason, the thought irritated me.

"We could have cared," Jack answered, as if I should have known. "Sometimes that's all it takes."

"Life is that simple?" I challenged.

"Life isn't simple," Jack replied. "Life is twisted and complicated and sometimes very messy. But a little care can go a long way in helping a guy negotiate the obstacles."

"This guy needed a lot more than a little care," I said, again with an edge. "This guy needed . . . " I didn't know how to finish the sentence.

"A lot of care?" Merl suggested.

"Yeah, a whole lot of care, and maybe a new start, and who knows what all." I was frustrated by the simplistic mindset I was hearing. In retrospect, there was nothing they were saying that should have upset me. I think my frustration at the time was part of the more general frustration I was walking around in 24/7.

"I think I can understand why you're so upset." The observation came from Jack. I hoped simplicity was not being replaced by psychoanalysis.

"What do you mean?" I responded — before I realized that this was the exact response I didn't want to make.

"When you think about it, there's a lot that you and that young fellow had in common. Both loners, both on the road, probably both running from a bunch of mistakes." Empathy had changed to prying.

"You sure seem to think you know a lot about both of us." I was getting a little angry. Everything felt strange. It was like someone had just stuck their fist into my gut and given a big twist. I felt like I was going to throw up again.

"He didn't need to die," Jack said.

The brothers both got up and headed inside. I had the feeling that they wanted to talk more about what was going on with me but wouldn't press it until I opened the door. I sat for a while and watched the shadows on the lake slowly usher in the twilight. As the shock began to wear off, I wondered why the suicide had shaken me up so much. Obviously, the sight of splattering brain matter is enough to unnerve the best of men. But what I had experienced was something else. It felt personal. It was as if I were watching myself, or some unresolved version of myself, pulling the trigger. Hopelessness. Was that where I was heading?

When I finally headed inside, I found Merl at work in the kitchen and Jack sitting in the reading area, poring over what appeared to be an extremely old book. I sat in Merl's chair, opposite him. "That looks pretty old," I said.

"Very," Jack said with a smile. "It's my personal favorite of all the books."

"What is it?"

"The New Testament," he said nonchalantly. "In Greek."

"How old?" I asked.

"Twelfth or thirteenth century is the best guess."

"You've got to be kidding!" I said.

"Here, take a look." He handed me the volume.

"What were you reading?" I asked.

"Gospel of John."

I looked at the hand-copied pages. There in bold pen strokes the Greek text jumped off the page: *En arche hen ho logos*. It was from the first chapter of John, the famous logos passage. "This is amazing," I said.

"I love reading the old manuscripts," he said.

"Where did you get this?"

"Ephesus," he answered, as if he just said "Cleveland."

"How . . . ?"

"It's a long story," was all he said.

I flipped through several pages until I came to the words: "*Ean tis dipsa, erchestho pros me kai pineto.*"

"If anyone thirsts," I said aloud. "I guess that kid needed a drink of what Jesus offered here."

"Who doesn't?" Jack said.

Before I could respond, Merl called from the kitchen, "Let's eat!"

The meal began with the blessing by Merl. It was delivered, as Jack had the night before, with great feeling.

"Do you mind if I ask a very personal question?" I said.

"Not at all," Merl answered for both.

"Do you actually believe all you just prayed?"

The brothers looked at each other. Jack took the lead. "Let me ask you a question," he said.

"Shoot," I said.

"You read Greek and Hebrew?"

"Yes."

"You have read and studied the New Testament and the Hebrew Scriptures of the Old Testament?"

"Correct again."

"What's not to believe?"

The question threw me. It wasn't the approach I had expected. "I guess you could nitpick about Joshua stopping the sun or where Cain got a wife," I said. "But I'd have to confess that most of the important data has been historically verified as accurate."

"I think what Jack wants to know is a bit more personal. What's not to believe, for you?" Merl asked.

I thought for a few minutes. This was at the heart of my dilemma. "I don't know. Rationally, and empirically, I think I still believe it's true."

"But?" Jack said.

"But experientially, and personally, and viscerally, and whatever other words you want to use for the pragmatic side of things, I don't think it works," I confessed.

"Excellent!" Merl exclaimed, looking at Jack.

I was quiet for a moment. "That's a pretty strange response to what I've just told you," I said.

"I'm just glad we know where things stand. You have a wonderful problem," Jack said.

"How do you figure?" I asked, a bit confused.

"You need a shot of reality!" Merl exclaimed. "That's probably why you were led here!"

Not knowing what to say, I started in on the dinner Merl had prepared — a lamb dish with an herb sauce that had a bittersweet taste. The homemade bread was unleavened to go with the Passover motif. "Is this my Last Supper?" I asked jokingly.

"We eat this meal in remembrance of our release from slavery and the fact that death has passed us over," Merl said with the casual air of one talking about tomorrow's weather forecast.

"You guys are unbelievable."

"What's not to believe?" Jack said with a serious look. Before I could respond, he grinned. "Gotcha! Here, have another piece of matzo."

After dinner, we went outside again and sat on the deck. The stars had come out, and the small gas lanterns the brothers had installed cast dancing shadows around the deck. The three of us sat quietly and gazed at the stars. It was beautiful. After a while, Merl said, "John, I have an idea."

"What's that?" I asked.

"We have this group that's like an extended family. We get together every week for singing and prayer and usually a little teaching," he said. "I guess you could say it's our church."

"Why don't you come with us?" Jack asked.

"When?" I asked.

"Tomorrow night, over at the Grange Hall outside of town," Merl said.

"I don't think your part will come in tomorrow," Jack added.

"I'm not sure I'm up for church at the moment," I said. I had mixed feelings. The events of the day had thrown me into a place I had not experienced in the last few years. Part of me was really looking hard at all that had happened and what it felt like in relation to my life. Part of me was still fighting the thought that maybe what I was looking for would take me back to a place I'd already been and found intolerable. The brothers didn't push.

"Well, think about it," Merl said. "I think you might find it interesting."

"I'll give it some thought," I said.

9

Somewhere Fast

Journal — September 20: *I saw a human being blow his brains out yesterday. For a moment, I thought he was going to blow mine out — that it was all over. I am in desperate shape. I feel like I'm in the middle of a lake covered with fog, sitting in a rowboat without an oar. I know the shore is out there, but I can't figure out which direction it is or how to get there. Nothing is working. I need help.*

"Brothers and sisters, welcome to church!" His name was Jake, and the accent and dreadlocks were distinctly Jamaican. No sooner were the words out of his mouth than the band began to crank. The music was really good. I found out later that a couple of the guys in the band had been studio musicians. I was intrigued by the collection of people gathered in the Grange Hall and the joyful enthusiasm of the group. It certainly didn't feel like church — at least as I knew it.

I had spent most of the day resisting taking the brothers up on their invitation. What I really wanted to do was to spend the night at a bar and meet someone who might make me reconsider my self-imposed celibacy.

I once heard someone say that it is truly remarkable just how wrong some people can be when they really put their mind to it. A bar and a woman were the last things I needed in my current state, but like most men, they were the first things I thought of. That in itself wasn't so amazing; *what was* amazing was that I was actually aware that this would not be helpful. That realization might have been aided by the fact that there was no bar anywhere near the brother's cabin — and I hadn't seen a really good-looking woman since I'd arrived in St. Johns.

I'd helped Merl in the diner all day, and it wasn't until about five in the afternoon that Jack came over and asked me again if I wanted to join them.

"I really don't want to be pushy," he said. "If you don't want to come, don't. You won't offend us."

"If what you have told us about your past church experience is true," Merl said, "you might not find what we do to be anything at all like church."

It was decision time, and I really was about 50/50. I said, "Okay. But if I walk out during the service, don't get mad."

"Mad?" said Jack. "Shoot, if you walk out during the service we'll just assume it made you so sick you had to go throw up!"

He tried to say it sincerely but couldn't hold a straight face.

"Heck," I said. "If it gets that bad, I might just spew right there in the Grange Hall!"

I had arrived with the brothers relatively early since both Merl and Jack seemed to play leadership roles in the group. They simply called it the fellowship. The Grange Hall was a few miles down Highway 61 from the brothers' cabin. As people got out of their cars in the parking lot, it became obvious that this was not your normal rural Arizona crowd. There were longhairs, shorthairs, some coat and ties, some bikers; you name it, this group had it all. The one characteristic that seemed to pervade the entire group was a visible excitement at being here and seeing one another.

By about the third song, the place was jammed and jamming. I sat between Merl and Jack, but we didn't sit for long. Soon, everyone was on their feet, and some of the group had their hands in the air like some Pentecostal revival meeting. With this group, it seemed natural and uncontrived. It felt like an authentic lifting of holy hands unto the Lord. I kept mine down.

The music lasted a solid half hour, beginning with flat-out rock-and-roll, then progressively mellowing to softer songs expressing love for God and thanksgiving for his goodness. As the singing came to an end, many heads were either bowed in prayer or lifted upward in silent reverie.

The quiet was broken by a voice from the stage: "Thanks! I needed that." I had met the speaker when we'd first arrived. Jack and Merl called him Doc, but I heard others call him Bob. In his early fifties, he was balding and gray, with hair pulled back in a ponytail that fell about a foot down his back. Like many others in the room, he had that Arizona look — faded jeans, cowboy boots, a simple cotton shirt, and a belt with a silver-and-turquoise buckle.

"Let's take a minute and say hi to any visitors," Bob said.

Merl stood and said, "This is our new friend John. His Harley broke down, and he's staying with us for a few days."

I appreciated the simplicity. Several others stood and introduced visiting family or neighbors or work associates who were at the fellowship for the first time. After the introductions, Bob asked if there was anything people wanted to pray about together. Several of the group stood and shared needs in their own lives or in the life of a family member or friend.

"You probably heard about the young fellow who blew his

brains out up at the reservoir yesterday," Merl said. "I don't know if he had a family or wife or anything, but we ought to pray for that situation."

Several other people voiced concerns they wanted the group to pray for. One of the men in the band was asked to come and lead the group in corporate prayer. A number of people from the group spontaneously offered short prayers out loud, and when all had been quiet for a few minutes, the guy from the band simply said, "That's it, Father." He sat down, and Bob walked up to a small, wooden podium, opening his Bible as he came.

"I was planning on teaching on another subject tonight," he began, in a relaxed and casual manner, "but I haven't been able to stop thinking about this young fellow who took his life over at the reservoir yesterday."

I hadn't been able to shake it either. Of course, seeing the whole thing in living color was a bit different from hearing about it secondhand.

"None of us really knows a thing about this young guy, but you have to wonder what went wrong."

My exact thoughts.

"We don't know if he had a wife. We don't know if he had any kids. We don't know if his mother and father are still living. All we know is that life became so intolerable for this fellow that the most logical solution he could think of was to put a Smith and Wesson in his mouth and blow the top of his head off."

The room was very quiet.

"Most of us here are familiar with the story of the prodigal son. For some reason, this is the story that keeps coming to mind when I think about the suicide. The story is found in the gospel of Luke, chapter fifteen. I've been processing the story from a little different viewpoint than I usually do when I think about the prodigal. We all know that it's primarily a story about God as father. It's a story about grace and forgiveness. I think it may be my favorite story Jesus told. I guess I've always related to the prodigal, although in my mature years I fear that I have too often become more like the anal-retentive brother."

A gentle laughter came from the group.

I remembered going through that same transition. I had been pretty rowdy before my conversion and seminary days, but integration into the organized church and all that went along with membership in the clergy required that you fit certain expected norms. That had been part of what drove me crazy.

"What I found myself thinking about," he continued, "were the choices the prodigal made that first took him away from home, and then the ones that led him back. I keep thinking about choices and decisions, and how they shape the course of our lives—either for good, or for disaster.

"The story of the prodigal begins with what was obviously a bad choice. Since he wasn't old enough to actually have his inheritance, he must have been relatively young and naive.

Dad has cash. The son is going to get it, eventually, but delayed gratification is not his style. He goes to Dad and demands it now. Obviously, this is a parable, because most Jewish dads in Jesus' time would probably have disinherited him on the spot and then had the tar beaten out of him. The father's capitulation to the son's demands is part of what makes the parable so scandalous.

"Then the son chooses to leave home: another bad decision. I'm not saying that we should never sever the umbilical cord, but in this situation, there was probably a great deal to be gained by hanging around Dad for a while longer. My hunch is that when it was the right time to leave, Dad would let you know.

"The prodigal goes to a foreign land, which might be another bad choice — hard to say. For sure, he chooses some bad friends and blows his dough on a long string of questionable expenditures. Bad choice, after bad choice, after bad choice, after bad choice, until he ends up in a pigpen.

"Since I know most of you pretty well, and most of you know me pretty well, I will apologize to our visitors today for including them in the following generalization — most of us know about the pigpen."

There was a general murmuring of affirmation in the group.

"Most of us have been in the pigpen. It wasn't the same pigpen for each of us, but nonetheless, it was a pigpen. There is always a pigpen at the end of the road marked 'Bad Choices.'

"Some of you were in a pigpen that you found inside a bottle. Some of us didn't know it was a pigpen because we were so wasted on drugs we didn't have a clue where we were. Some of our pigpens were in beautiful parts of the city and came with country-club memberships. Bad choices, selfish choices, lead to pigpens.

"All this is pretty familiar turf to us. The thing I began to think about was what a miracle it was that the prodigal ever got out of the pigpen. Some people never do. I think the young man at the reservoir was so deep in the muck of the pigpen that he had no clue how to get out.

"So I found myself wondering: What was the difference between the prodigal and the guy at the reservoir? The prodigal had someplace to go, and the dude who is now dead didn't? The prodigal had a family that wanted him back, and our dead friend didn't? I think you can come up with a whole lot of reasons why the prodigal had it better than the drifter, but I came to the conclusion that the bottom line is another choice. The prodigal finally made a good choice, and the guy over at Zion made his last bad one."

As Bob spoke, I reflected on the choices I had made over the last five years. Then I thought back to the choices I had made before that—the ones that got me into the situation that led to the more recent bad choices. I thought about my quest to find some kind of an answer—and the thought slowly began to take hold of me that maybe all I needed was to make a choice. I passed this off as too simplistic an answer.

"Choices are all we really have in life. They are the most sacred actions we take. I think this is what Paul meant when he encouraged the Romans to offer themselves as living sacrifices. The text says that this is our *logidzomai* act of worship. You can translate that word a number of ways, but what Paul seems to be saying is that authentic worship isn't made up of religious ritual, but of logical decisions that constitute multiple acts of worship. The prodigal didn't get an epiphany. Neither did the guy at the lake. What they each got was a clarifying moment — a point in time and space when a choice had to be made.

"Now, before I go further, let me say that I am a big believer in divine intervention. I believe that God is always performing gracious interventions. But as I thought about our young man at the reservoir, I found myself internally having the old debate about how intervention fits with the sovereignty of God and the freedom of man. I won't pretend that I can resolve that one tonight, but what if it is in that moment of decision that God intervenes? The whole debate on election and freedom hinges on this. Do we freely choose, or is even the ability to choose a gift of grace? Here's what I'm getting at. I'm convinced that I never would have given my life to God if he hadn't done something that enabled me to give myself. But when push came to shove, it was still a matter of choice. I was confronted with the reality of Christ and told I had to make a decision. I could reject or neglect, or I could surrender and give myself to him. I struggled like crazy, until I had that moment of clarity when I knew that Jesus was real and alive and offering me a life, and I had to choose. I am convinced that as soon as I moved in the direction of the right choice, I was enabled. My hunch is that I was even nudged to move in that direction. But that might make me too much of a Calvinist for some of you."

The group seemed to get a small kick out of this.

Bob went on. "I think this is what happened to the prodigal. There he is, sitting in the pigpen. He has blown everything. Suddenly, or maybe as a climax to some period of reflection, the text says he 'came to his senses.' He has a rare moment of clarity. He has a choice. He can stay in the pigpen. He can steal a pig and run. He can kill the farmer and rape his wife and then steal a pig and run. Bad choices are always an option. Until you make the one the young guy did yesterday. Then your options are all played out. But in his moment of clarity, the prodigal sees the right choice. 'I could go home. I don't have to live like this any more. This is stupid. I am stupid.' And then, the critical moment. In an instant, he makes the choice — or begins to make the choice and gets enabled to make the choice. And shazam! The whole course of his life heads in a new direction. He begins making good choices. There didn't seem to be any bolts of lightning or supernatural appearances or anything out of the ordinary. He just came to his senses. Maybe that in itself is the miracle. And he ends up at the party with the ring and the robe and Dad's blessing.

"Yesterday, maybe that young guy had exactly the same kind of moment. Who knows? What if in a moment of clarity, he knew that he had a choice? He certainly knew he could choose to stick a gun in his mouth. That was a choice. But what if he was thinking, 'I could go home and ask for another chance.' Or, 'Maybe I should call Mom and ask for help.' Or even, 'Maybe I can hang on one more day.' There were choices."

Bob stopped for a moment and hung his head. He had been speaking with incredible intensity. After a moment he took a big breath, looked up and smiled.

"Brother . . . I'm way too intense tonight." The crowd seemed relieved. It had been a shared intensity. "I need to wrap this up. Here's the point. We're all making choices in our lives. Some of you might be making bad ones. Some of you might be considering choices that will put you in the pigpen. Some of you might be there already. Here is what I think God wants to say to you and me tonight: 'Choose me. Choose the right thing. Choose the good thing. Come back home.'

"I think it's just that simple." He paused for a minute, looking out at the faces of the men and women in the audience. Then he said, "Let's pray silently for a few minutes. Try and get a read on what God might want to say to you tonight."

Everyone in the room bowed their head. I heard some praying in murmurs or whispers. After a minute, I heard several people crying. Obviously, the message had hit home. I knew it had been on target for me. I had been in the pigpen for at least five years, probably more like ten. I had made so many bad choices, I wasn't sure I knew how to make a good one. I bowed my head, not expecting much. That's when it happened.

Whatever you do, don't stop reading now. You might not like what I say, but I promise, it really happened like this. I'm still uncertain how to describe it. I remember both Wolf and Flaherty saying that the best things are hard to articulate.

I began to have some kind of encounter with God. It wasn't as dramatic as Wolf's experience of rolling around in the woods — although some of Wolf's language seemed to fit. I felt something happening. I was somehow being touched. I had the sense that somehow God was there, which was ironic, given that for five years I had been — experientially, at least — questioning his existence. Suddenly, all of that seemed amazingly foolish.

This sense of presence started to bring my actions into focus. It started with Teddy. In my mind I could see Teddy, over and over again, crying as I'd left him time after time. I began to grasp something of the intensity of the pain I had inflicted on my little boy. I began to cry. First Jack, then Merl, placed a hand on my back. Later, I realized that they were probably just asking God to get me real good.

Then came an image of Stephanie. It wasn't as if I were getting technicolor instant replays projected in front of me; rather, it was internal. I could see her in my mind. I could see the anger in her eyes. I could hear her voice as she told me how much she hated me. And then I sensed her pain. It was deeper and stronger than Teddy's. Something at the core of her being had been horribly wounded by what I had done. My crying turned to weeping. I would have been embarrassed if I had been at all conscious of the other people sitting in the room, but I was oblivious to anything other than the experience itself.

I remembered holding her on the day she was born, and then I thought about her pain again. My weeping grew more intense. I slid out of my chair to my knees in emotional agony. I could feel more hands being placed on me, and I could hear the gentle murmur of people praying.

Then the worst came. My thoughts turned to Elizabeth. I envisioned her the day we met. She was such a beautiful woman with this amazingly sweet spirit and complete trust in me. She had been given to me as a gift. And I had been given to her. That was what marriage was supposed to be: a man and a woman, wounded by the experiences of living in a fallen world, are given to each other to heal each other's wounds. Instead, I had wounded her: every careless word, every critical attitude — pain inflicted on the one who was to heal my pain with her love and who I was to heal with mine. Then I remembered her face the day I left. I imagined what she must have felt, and it was as if a searing iron were slowly twisting in my heart.

I dropped from my knees to my face, convulsed in emotional and spiritual pain. What had I done? I remembered the words of the Jesus Prayer, "Lord Jesus Christ, have mercy on me, a sinner." I prayed the words.

I continued to weep. I felt guilt of immense proportion. I kept saying, "I'm so sorry. I'm so sorry." It was all that would come out, and it was directed at people who weren't even there to hear it.

I cried until I couldn't cry any longer. That is when I began to have another kind of experience, even more difficult to put into words. The only way I can describe it is to say that it felt as if, at the core of my being, God was engaging me with the core of his being. I had never experienced anything like it in my life. I had known times of feeling close to God. I had certainly been through times of feeling distant. But nothing like this.

I believe I was having what St. John of the Cross would have called an experience of union. At the deepest level of my being, I began to feel what I can only describe as love. It started deep within and then seemed to flow through me and over me like a wave. I can't explain how I knew it was God, and you can dismiss it as some kind of psychological reaction to years of built-up guilt. I don't really care. I knew it was God. Then the two experiences coalesced: the pain I had felt — a pain I had inflicted on others — and now this sense of love. It should have seemed incongruous because logically it was. But then a word came to my mind: *grace*. When I put this together, I started to cry again. This time they were tears not of remorse but of gratitude. Please, don't write it off as cliché, but I knew that in all my failure, and even with all the pain I had inflicted, God was communicating to me that he loved me. This was why Jesus had died. He died for this. I deserved something horrible, but I got love.

I passed out.

When I regained consciousness, I was still lying on the floor. Only the brothers were there with me. They had been crying. Bob was sitting nearby with his head bowed, apparently praying.

"I don't know if I can get up," I said.

"You don't have to," Jack replied.

I stayed on the floor a few more minutes, saying nothing. When I felt I could, I sat up. "I'm not sure what just happened," I said, finally feeling back in possession of my faculties.

Jack, Merl, and Bob just looked at me without saying anything.

"What I mean is, I know exactly what just happened to me," I said, "but I don't have the ability to express it."

"Enlightened at last!" Merl exclaimed.

I sat silently for a second and then began to smile. "You're absolutely right!" I said. "I've just been enlightened."

On the trip back to the cabin, I alternately sat in complete silence or attempted to describe to the brothers what I had experienced during the service. They acted like it was no big deal — as if it should be considered the normative experience in any really good church service.

I quieted down as the awareness began to grow that what I had experienced required a response. Like the prodigal, I was still in the pigpen, even though I had somewhat "come to my senses." God had initiated something, and I needed to respond.

Back at the cabin, Merl said, "If all goes according to schedule, your chip could arrive tomorrow. Jack could have the Harley up and running by noon."

"Then I have to decide what to do next," I said. "And it had better be a really good decision."

"Hopefully, the first of many," Jack said.

"Let's all get a good night's sleep and work on this in the morning," Merl suggested.

I knew there was no way in the world I was going to be able to get to sleep, but the brothers looked beat, and I knew they would be up bright and early in the morning to head to work. We all went inside and said our goodnights. I lay awake for a long time, going over and over the events of the evening and what they might mean. I worked my way back to all that had happened in the last few years and began to see how all of it fit. All the struggle, all the failure, even all the bad choices had been a part of getting me to

St. Johns and the meeting at the Grange Hall. Again it's hard to explain, but it all fit. Eventually, I drifted off to sleep.

I awoke to the smell of freshly brewed coffee and the unmistakable pop and aroma of bacon frying. I would miss the warm hospitality I had enjoyed with the brothers, but I knew it was time to move on. I'd come up with a tentative plan sometime during the night — not very detailed, just a general direction. I felt a sense of resolve to get on with it.

Stumbling down the stairs, I found Jack and Merl deep in conversation at the kitchen table. The table was covered with yellow legal pads filled with notes, and plates of eggs, bacon, fresh fruit, and toast.

"Good morning," I said, startling them out of the intensity of their discussion.

"Good morning!" they exclaimed simultaneously.

"We're glad you're up," Jack said.

"We've been working all morning on a plan," Merl added. "Sit down, and eat some breakfast."

The brothers were visibly excited. I didn't know what they had cooked up, besides the eggs, but I had a feeling that it would be interesting.

"We've been scheming all morning on how to help you out," Jack said.

"You guys are great," I said, taking a bite of eggs. "But you've done enough. I'll never be able to repay you for your kindness. I think the time has come for me to take responsibility for my own life." The words scared me. Resolution was one thing; performance was another. I didn't have the world's greatest track record on the latter.

"Hogwash!" Merl exclaimed. "That's the kind of thinking that got you into trouble in the first place. If I had the time, I would explain to you how we are in this thing together, and everything we do to help you ends up helping us, too. It's how the system was designed to work."

"What's all this?" I asked, pointing to the yellow pads.

"Just some scribbling to try to figure out how to make our idea work."

"So what are you thinking this morning?" Jack asked.

"I know I have to change direction," I said.

"Away from LA?" Jack asked.

"Not physical direction, but it will involve that also. I need to get out of the pigpen. I have to figure out how to get back into relationship with my kids." The words flowed so smoothly that it was as if my voice was the instrument of another mind — at least another mind than the one that I had been using for the last five years.

"From what you've told us," Jack said, "in the case of your son that should be a relatively easy task. Your wife and daughter might be another story."

"Technically, I don't have a wife, and the one I don't technically have is about to get married," I said.

"I think from a theological-technical point of view, she is still technically your wife until she technically gets remarried," Merl said, with a bit of a mocking tone. "Let's at least throw the possibility of reconciliation into the equation."

It was something I hadn't even considered.

"Are you going to continue your trip?" Jack asked.

"I think I'm just beginning my trip," I said.

"What direction are you going?" Merl asked.

"Down, I hope," was all I said.

As we ate breakfast, it became clear that the brothers had done a lot of thinking, and they weren't afraid to broach difficult subjects. Along with marital reconciliation, they reminded me of my new friend in Chicago whom I had promised a call as soon as I found what I was looking for. They also cautioned me about not getting my hopes too high for immediate resolution. It had taken years to dig the hole I was in, and it might take some time to fix things.

I told them what I had come up with before I fell asleep. "I don't have the details firmly in place, but as soon as the Harley is running, I'm heading back to Albuquerque. I figure my best shot at beginning to get things right is to concentrate on being a dad for Teddy. I know I hurt him when I left last time, but he's the most forgiving of the family. I honestly believe that if I tell him what happened out here and ask for his forgiveness, he'll give me a break."

"Then what?" asked Merl.

"I don't know what to think about Elizabeth," I said. "But I want to be there for Teddy. I think I'll stay in Albuquerque and get a job. I don't care if I have to work at McDonald's or 7-Eleven. I'm going to go be with my son.

"I need to think about Elizabeth. I don't want to sabotage her pending wedding. But if I'm there, maybe something could develop, if it's supposed to. My greatest concern is Stephanie, and quite frankly, I don't have a clue what to do about her."

"That'll be a tough one," Merl agreed.

"We've been thinking," Jack said. "We might have a way to help you accomplish your plans."

"Let's head into town and talk there," Jack added. "Some of what we're thinking might make more sense there. Also, if FedEx has been able to find us, your chip ought to be in."

I had intended to pack my bags and take them with me, figuring that if Jack got the bike running I might head out for Albuquerque that afternoon. Merl convinced me to stay at least one more night so that we could have a nice going-away dinner. Jack suggested that we kill the fatted calf. Actually, the fatted calf had already been killed and stuck in Merl and Jack's freezer. Merl said he would thaw some out and throw it on the grill. It sounded like the perfect meal to go with the prodigal son motif.

I had grown so attached to these two guys in such a short time that I got a bit emotional riding between them into town, thinking that after tomorrow, I might never see them again. It made me realize how much their care and love meant to me. Being with them seemed so right — but I knew that being with my son would be even better.

It was late morning by the time we hit the diner. I went inside with Merl while Jack walked across to the station to see if the part had arrived. He joined us a few minutes later. "I have some good news and some bad news," he said as he walked in.

"Good news first," I said.

"The chip has arrived."

"And the bad news?"

"In Phoenix."

"Will it be here today?"

"Late," Jack said. "I think the bike will be ready in the morning."

"Great," I said.

"Want to hear our ideas?" Merl asked.

"Absolutely," I said.

We sat down in a booth and Jack began, "Merl and I would like to make you a proposition."

"I'm open to just about anything," I said.

"We want you to consider coming here to live with us for a while."

I was taken off guard, and had to think for a few seconds before I responded. "It's wonderful of you to suggest it, but I can't."

"Why not?" Merl asked.

"I have a son in Albuquerque who needs a dad."

"Bring him here," Merl said. "There are good schools, and the lifestyle is wholesome."

"He could help me out at the station, and I could teach him to work on motorcycles," Jack said.

"If he didn't enjoy doing that, I could teach him to cook," Merl said.

"That's a very generous offer," I said. "I don't think Elizabeth will buy it, though."

"It'll take time, I'm sure," Jack said. "But you could transition into it as Elizabeth gains confidence in you."

"Could be a win/win," Merl said. "You'd be a tremendous help to us, and we think we might be able to help you."

"I'm sure you could," I said. I smiled, then quoted Father Flaherty's explanation of Romans chapter seven: "I need all the help I can get."

"We think this is a pretty special place," Merl said. "When you told us about what that priest in Albuquerque suggested, we began to think that this might be a good place for you to get some time to make transitions."

"We also think our friendship could be a help," Jack said. "Draw that diagram you told us about, and I'll show you what I mean."

I grabbed a napkin out of the holder and drew a quick "ascent, crisis, and descent" schematic.

Jack pointed to the Holy Fool area of the diagram and said, "We're really close to that elder age, you know." He was joking, but the fact was, the brothers were as close to Holy Fools as anyone I'd ever met, including Leppick, Monroe, and Wolf.

"You need time," Merl said. "If I had to put your experience on this drawing, I'd say you are right at the juncture where the three lines leave the far side of that crisis circle." He took a knife and pointed to the intersection point where the Old Fool, Bitter Old Man, and Wisdom Journey lines began. I took my pen and drew all three in with an X at the place he was pointing to.

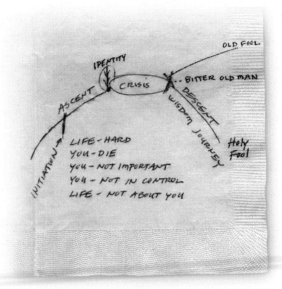

"You'll also need support and stability to make the next part of your journey," Jack said.

"Who knows, you might even want to do a little teaching at the fellowship. Bob could use a little help," Merl suggested.

"I don't know about —"

"No, wait a minute," Jack said. "I know what you're going to say. You think you fouled things up beyond salvage and that you aren't ever going to do anything in a church again. Right?"

"Something like that."

"You're wrong. And once again, that's the kind of thinking that got you into trouble," Jack said. "This is a fresh start. You need to make some amends, but your failure is behind you, and certainly behind God. You are a trained and gifted communicator of the most important message in the universe. You were not named John Calvin by chance. The world needs a new Reformation. You can be part of it. St. Johns is no more obscure than Wittenberg. You can speak, teach, and write, and you can help Bob pastor that little fellowship of great people where God touched your life."

❀

I needed some time to think about all the brothers had laid out. I needed to figure out how I could stay with them and still be a dad to Teddy. I knew Elizabeth wouldn't let him come to Arizona for any lengthy period of time, if at all. He was still too young for that. I did think she might let him come for a few days at a time when school was out or on vacations. I also figured that I could make the trip to Albuquerque regularly. If I pushed the Harley, I could get there in under four hours. I was sure it would take quite a few trial runs to give Elizabeth confidence that my intentions were good and that I was committed to Teddy. If commuting didn't work, I could still move to Albuquerque and find a job.

I thought about all this while helping the guys out at the diner and the station. About four in the afternoon, FedEx delivered the chip. Jack started working on it immediately, promising that the bike would be ready by morning. He also said that he and Merl had one other item they wanted to run by me but that they would wait till dinner.

"Father, we are grateful tonight for your love and care and provision," Jack prayed. Again, he was standing at the table holding a loaf of fresh-baked bread up toward God. "And we especially give you thanks for bringing John here and all you are doing and are going to do in his life."

"Amen," Merl said.

"Amen," I added.

Merl served the meal, and as we ate, the brothers began to reveal the final piece of their plan.

"For some time now, Merl and I have been wanting to take a little break," Jack said.

"We've been talking about riding to LA on our scooters for the last several years and have never been able to break away from here to do it," Merl said. "You, of all people, can probably appreciate what we have been thinking. We want to ride as much of old Route 66 between here and the end of Santa Monica Pier as we can."

"The tales of your journey have rekindled that desire," Jack said. "If you would run the diner, there would only be one obstacle that is still in our way."

"What's that?" I asked.

"I'm in great shape for the trip," Merl said. "My Ultra is the perfect piece of machinery for this kind of adventure. But Jack has a problem, even if he won't admit it."

"Merl is convinced that my old FL isn't up for a trip of that magnitude. I have attempted to assure him that I will take the necessary tools to keep it running, but he has convinced me that there is a better option."

"Which is?" I asked.

"I have to confess that from the minute you pulled into the station, I have been thinking how great it would be if Jack had something like your Road King to take on the trip," Merl said. "I was thinking that maybe we could make a trade of unlimited room and board for the limited use of your Harley."

"I would be honored," I said. "Doing anything to repay you in the smallest way would mean a lot to me."

"We wouldn't leave you without transportation," Jack said. "You would also have unlimited use of the Jeep."

"I think it would make it to Albuquerque without any trouble if you decide to head that way while we're gone," Merl said.

"You can also use the FL whenever you want, but you shouldn't try to ride it all the way to Albuquerque," Jack added.

"Bob has already committed to cover the station while we're gone. When you need to go to Albuquerque, Jake could handle the diner," Merl said.

I laughed at the picture of Jake with his dreadlocks and Jamaican accent welcoming people as they came in the door, "Brothers and sisters, what can I get you today?"

By the end of dinner, the plan was in place. It seemed a little crazy, but I had this funny feeling that it actually might work. Every time I brought up some potential problem, Jack reminded me of the words Jesus spoke to Julian of Norwich in her fourteenth-century "showing": "All shall be well, and all will be well, and all manner of things shall be well."

It was another gorgeous fall morning in Arizona. We had driven to the station to meet Bob and Jake before Merl and Jack hit the road. It didn't take long to pack the bikes; the brothers were traveling light. They looked great in their classic leather motorcycle jackets and leather chaps. Both had their hair pulled back in ponytails and wore shorty helmets. The scene of them sitting on the Harleys, ready to hit the road, looked like a Harley-Davidson Christmas card with Santa in stereo.

"When do you think you'll be back?" I finally remembered to ask.

The brothers looked at each other. "I hadn't even thought about it," Jack said.

"Don't worry," Merl said. "We'll keep in touch. And we'll let you know how to get in touch with us."

Like everything else they did, the brothers fired up their bikes almost simultaneously. The rumble of the muffler system I had installed on the Road King brought a tinge of envy. Part of me wished I were heading west with them. I walked over to Merl and gave him a hug, then did the same to Jack.

"I love you guys," I choked out.

Jack reached out and pulled me into a hug, then kissed my forehead. They hit their shift pegs at the same time and gave the bikes a twist of the throttles. The two headed out the exit of Fat Bobs. Merl shouted something back across his shoulder as he held his left hand high. I couldn't quite make out the words, but I thought they sounded Celtic. All I know is that as they reached my ears, I felt warmth flow over my body and a sense that everything would be all right.

I watched the two head up the highway toward old Route 66 till both were out of sight.

Postscript

I often think back to that morning at Fat Bobs and all that has happened since. Things haven't gone quite as I anticipated. The brothers tell me that recognizing that you're not in control is one of the big lessons of the descent. It was my intention to head back to Albuquerque as soon as possible to be with Teddy. I called Elizabeth, and she hung up. I called again, and she hung up again. When I called the third time, she told me to quit calling, and that if I didn't, she was going to call the police and tell them I was harassing her. I decided I'd better give things a little more time. I began to write to her and Teddy, attempting to explain what had happened. I didn't hear back from Elizabeth for a few weeks, but Teddy began to write immediately.

In the meantime, I kept the diner going while the brothers were away. I discovered that I like cooking. The obsessive part of my personality also finds some degree of pleasure in attempting to keep the place as spotless as Merl did.

I started trying to live in a way that reflected my desire to respond appropriately to what had happened at the Grange Hall.

I don't know what I thought that would be like, but it has been more challenging than I could have imagined. In some ways, I made a one-hundred-and-eighty-degree turn that night. But even with divine intervention, some habits die hard.

The brothers have been wonderful. They had a great trip and came home with story after story of amazing encounters along the way. They've been guiding me on my exit from the pigpen and coming to terms with the crisis. They have helped me understand that the spiritual journey is much more challenging than the religious life most folks settle for. It is one thing to talk about a false identity and taking the Wisdom Journey toward becoming a Holy Fool. The reality is that coming to terms with the things in our life that are false, and turning from the faulty ways of thinking with which we have been programmed, is difficult. Merl and Jack have encouraged me that it doesn't happen quickly. They think I'm pretty young to be worrying about it anyway and keep reminding me I have thirty or forty years to get it right.

After weeks of letters, Elizabeth finally agreed to begin talking. Eventually, she gave me the green light to come see Teddy. By then, the weather in New Mexico was too shaky to be riding the Harley, so I took the old Jeep. The truck did amazingly well, although I did need to replace the fuel pump in Gallup.

Elizabeth was rightfully skeptical for some time. Eventually, she agreed to a trial run with Teddy. He has been out several times for short visits. He loves St. Johns, and the brothers are now

"Uncle Merl" and "Uncle Jack." He has learned to flip a burger and do an oil change.

I didn't have the heart to say anything to Elizabeth about the brothers' idea of reconciliation. I decided to pray about it and see what God might have up his sleeve. The wedding to Max has been postponed three times, so maybe the reports from Teddy have her wondering.

I waited a week to call Nikki. I gave her the whole story, both barrels blazing. I could tell she wasn't sure what to make of some of it, but she did invite me to come to Chicago, immediately. This was one of those really hard moments. I wanted to say yes but had the sense that it would be a mistake. I told her I was going to try to reconcile with Elizabeth. She said the good ones always get away.

I've been praying and reading the Bible. I have access to all the brothers' books and am enjoying getting to know God all over again. I was reading Philippians in their Greek New Testament the other day and pondering the text that says God is at work in us both to have the desire to do his will and to enable us to do it. I'm trusting in that statement one day at a time and working real hard to get it right.

I've started doing a little teaching at the church. Some have told me that they find it helpful. I've also started writing again. I thought I might try to do something along the lines of a modern-day *The Way of a Pilgrim*. I write early in the morning before Merl and Jack get up. I've set up a small desk in a corner of the living room with a view across the lake. Often, I find myself simply sitting looking across the water as the sun comes up, reflecting on the goodness of the new life I have been given.

I have even come up with my own version of the Jesus Prayer. I find myself repeating frequently, "Lord Jesus Christ, thank you for having mercy on me."

Author

DR. BOB BELTZ is the director of special projects for The Anschutz Corporation of Denver, Colorado. In this role Bob works as a consultant on film, television, and related projects designed to have a positive impact on popular culture.

As part of his work with The Anschuz Corporation, Bob is part of the development and production teams of Walden Media and Bristol Bay Productions. He served as co-producer of the movie *Joshua*, based on the best-selling book by Joe Girzone. He is currently working on a number of films including the live action version of *The Lion, the Witch and the Wardrobe* (coming December 9, 2005) and a film on the life of the great British reformer William Wilberforce.

Bob is an ordained Presbyterian minister. He served as the senior pastor of High Street Community Church, in Santa Cruz, California, and was one of the founding pastors of Cherry Hills Community Church in Highlands Ranch, Colorado, where he served for fifteen years as the teaching pastor. Along with his work in film, he still travels as a local and national speaker and teacher.

Bob is the author of ten books, including *The Solomon Syndrome*, *Becoming a Man of Prayer*, and the best-selling Daily *Disciplines for the Christian Man*. *Somewhere Fast* is his first novel.

Bob graduated from the University of Missouri in 1972 with a BA degree in economics. He received both his MA degree in biblical studies and his Doctor of Ministry in pastoral theology from Denver Seminary, Denver, Colorado.

Bob and his wife of thirty years, Allison, live in Littleton, Colorado. They have two children: a daughter Stephanie and a son Baker.

She came to conquer a king

but discovered a man and,

in the end, saved a nation.

Chosen

GINGER GARRETT

1-57683-651-7

What really happened in Xerxes' palace? Queen Esther's secret diaries tell all. Few knew she kept a private scroll of her deepest thoughts. From her days as a poor market wench through her rise to queen, she recorded it all—the sights and scandals—hoping that one day, others would learn the truth.

Visit your local Christian bookstore, call NavPress at 1-800-366-7788, or log on to www.navpress.com to purchase.

To locate a Christian bookstore near you, call 1-800-991-7747.

NAVPRESS ®
BRINGING TRUTH TO LIFE
www.navpress.com